DENNIS

THE MAN WITHOUT A HEAD

AND OTHER SHORT STORIES

STEVYN
EMBRACE THE
WEIRD STUFF!
(YOU ALREADY DO)
X D

A CURIOUS CROW PUBLICATION

This is a work of fiction. Any resemblance to actual persons, living, dead, or transformed beyond recognition, is entirely coincidental. Historical figures have been handled with care. Cows, dogs, and budgies cannot sue.

First Edition: 2025

ISBN 978 1 0369 6292 0

For permissions, objections, or to report strange transformations after reading, contact:
dennism40@hotmail.com

Your Journey

The Salt Water Garglers of Cill na Seacht nIníon

The Atlantic wind was battering all sorts of crap out of the ship's bell outside the Wren's Nest. The cliff-edge pub, with its crooked chimney, coughed peat smoke into the gale. Inside, the fire roared. The stout flowed. The talk jostled warm and loud. This was Cill na Seacht nIníon—or, if you believe the postcards, the Church of the Seven Daughters.

Near the fire sat Tadhg O'Shea, fisherman and joker, one boot off, watching the steam curl from his sock. He took a gulp of Guinness, then coughed and sneezed—a wet, phlegmy *phffftoooarghhhhgahhhhzz*, half walrus honk, half dying accordion. A glistening snot bubble ballooned from his nostril, wobbled, then dropped.

Seamus roared, "Jesus, Tadhg, that was nearly 'The Wild Rover.' Bet you can't gargle it with seawater." He thumped a whiskey jar of Atlantic brine on the counter, dragged in that morning as some half-baked hangover cure.

Tadhg smeared the bubble across his jersey, eyes gleaming now. He stood, raised the jar with a nod at Seamus, and, with a showman's grin, took a hefty swig. Then he began to gargle.

It sounded like a pig caught in a briar—high, jagged squeals. He hacked, spat a mist of salt across a table, then tried again: short, choking gulps, bubbles sliding from his lips. At last, a note rose like a seagull's cry, and the pub fell silent. "Sure, he's cracked in the head," Mairead, the proprietress, shouted, "but listen to that for a bit of craic!"

Tadhg hooked his arm through Seamus's and yanked him off the stool. "Come on with me, ye fecker." Seamus staggered upright, muttered a slurred pact, and they both swigged from the seawater jug.

Together they lurched into "The Fields of Athenry"—Tadhg squealing sharp above Seamus's gravelly rumble. One song bled into another until the two of them strangled out the last notes of "Danny Boy." By then the pub was stamping, clapping, and shouting for more, pint glasses drumming the tables.

That Thursday night did not end at closing time. Word spread, and before long half the island had crammed into the Wren's Nest for the salt-water singing. One after another, locals begged to try, spluttering and howling until the prank began to feel like a half-mad tradition.

Among the new recruits was Siobhan McCarthy, her soaring soprano long wasted on the church's half-hearted congregation; she lent an eerie beauty to "Mo Ghile Mear." Then lanky Padraig O'Driscoll—barely seventeen, quick with a tune—turned "The Rocky Road to Dublin" into a sloshing, choking spectacle equal parts melody and near-drowning.

And, in the corner, some swore they heard a whisper: that those who could match the sea's own music were fated for strange fortunes.

The Wren's Nest roared to life every Thursday. Farmers, fishermen, Aran knitters—even the priest—crammed shoulder to shoulder as the salt water garglers dipped their pint glasses into a barrel of Atlantic brine and let rip, spraying sea and song in equal measure. When the pub could hold no more, the crowd spilled into the yard and leaned against the stone walls, straining to catch the gargled mayhem.

Over Guinness and whiskey chasers, the group honed their briny ballads and argued the most pressing question of all: what in God's name were they going to call themselves?

"Na Gargálaithe Fairsinge!"

"Sounds like a bunch of feckin' monks, Siobhan—like we should be chantin' in Latin, not garglin' 'The Rocky Road to Dublin'!"

"Ah, but *fairsinge* has that poetic ring to it, Tadhg—'the vastness'—like the sea, deep and mysterious."

Padraig swallowed the last of his whiskey. "Aye, but it also sounds like a crowd of fellas who swallowed too much seawater and couldn't make it back to shore."

"Fine then, Padraig. What about 'Granolith Uisce Salann'?"

Seamus groaned. "Jesus, it sounds like a cure for a sore throat! Like somethin' your granny would make you drink when you're dyin' of the flu!"

After three more rounds of Guinness, two renditions of "The Fields of Athenry," and one failed attempt to gargle Beethoven's "Ode to Joy", Tadhg threw his hands in the air.

"Jaysus... We're the Salt Water Garglers! Simple as that. Or the Garglers."

The pub clapped its approval. The debate was settled, and so, with a clatter of glasses and laughter, the Salt Water Garglers were born.

Over the following Thursdays, Tadhg swapped his pint glass for a mason jar, swearing it gave him "a deeper, oceanic resonance".

Siobhan demanded seawater be drawn fresh each week from the cove beyond the headland where fishermen said the tide carried the whispers of lost voices. "The right salt content makes all the difference."

Padraig went further—dunking his head in a bucket before each performance. "Clears the throat, Seamus!" he spluttered, blinking through salt-stung eyes.

"It'll fill your feckin' lungs if you're not careful."

It was only a matter of time before the carry-ons at the Wren's Nest drew outside attention. The *Connemara Gazette* sent a junior reporter, Michael Hanrahan, to investigate the "peculiar musical talents" of Cill na Seacht nInión. On a damp Thursday evening, wedged in a corner with a dripping notebook, he watched the Garglers croak their way through "Carrickfergus". By the final chorus, he knew he had his front-page story.

Two days later, the headline blared from newsstands: *Ireland's Wettest Musicians*. Part praise, part bemusement, the piece struck a chord. The Garglers were no longer just a local oddity—they were folklore in the making.

Not long after Michael's article, a TV crew from Galway arrived to film the Garglers' take on "The Foggy Dew". The clip spread like wildfire—shared by grannies on Facebook before breakfast, passed round building sites by lunchtime—and by the weekend, Dublin had called. On *The Late Late Show*, they gargled "The Parting Glass" to a standing ovation.

Soon they were touring pubs and parish halls across the country. In Tralee, their briny harmonies earned roaring applause; in Wexford, an old man shouted, "That 'Danny Boy' was the best I've ever heard—and I've been listening to it since 1942!" One priest in Clare insisted they gargle "Ave Maria" with holy water and declared it "miraculous".

Galway was charmed, the isles were floored, but Belfast was another matter—a city that had cheered and booed in the same breath for generations.

The Crown Liquor Saloon was heaving, its mosaic floors sticky with stout, its stained-glass snugs spilling with voices. The audience was stiff and sceptical, pints half-drained but gripped tightly. The choice of song was not lost on anyone—"The Foggy Dew" carried a weight in Belfast that could sour a room as quick as it could stir it. Tadhg launched into it, Siobhan's voice rose like a ghost from the depths, Seamus's undertones rumbled through the floorboards, and slowly the din gave way. A man at the bar—who'd spent the first verse scowling into his Harp—paused mid-gulp and muttered,

"Well now, would ya listen to that..." In Belfast, the mutter was as good as a standing ovation.

Padraig closed the show with "The Rocky Road to Dublin", and the crowd rose as one, clapping and stomping for an encore. A lad near the front thumped his pint on the bar, froth sloshing over the rim, and bellowed, "Give them the keys to the city!"

In Dublin, they performed at Vicar Street to a packed house, the walls humming with conversation and clinking glasses. By the second song, a lad on the balcony was conducting the Garglers with his pint. A blonde-haired woman in the front row tilted her head back, took a giant swig of her vodka and Red Bull, and started gargling along in pure ecstasy. A group near the bar had started a slow, swaying embrace that had nothing to do with drink and everything to do with the rhythm.

Critics were split—some called them mad Irish geniuses, others brushed them off as "just a novelty act". One columnist wrote, "More spit than spectacle".

The Garglers remained unconcerned. The crowds loved them. They rode a wave of success—loud, messy, their own.

Their "Raglan Road" moved audiences to tears—not only because of the song's sadness but also because Seamus's deep baritone made it sound like the ghost of Patrick Kavanagh had stumbled into the pub, pint in hand, railing about lost love and bad luck.

They performed it in the Bailey, the spot where Kavanagh first handed the poem to Luke Kelly of The Dubliners, who gave it song and legend. Near the bar, a man in a scally cap swirled the last of his whiskey and muttered, "Kavanagh'd be sobbin' into his pint if he heard that." Their last song, "Irish Lullaby", was a soft farewell, floating through the crowd like a blessing, sending everyone home wrapped in a haze of song and stout.

Days blurred—long hauls, pints after encores, draughty B&Bs. Laughter outweighed quarrels, though Padraig pushed for new songs and Siobhan worried they were a novelty. Tadhg only laughed. "If it ain't broke, don't fix it," he'd say, raising his seawater jar.

In Ennis, a woman in a sequined cardigan pressed a rosary into Siobhan's hand, saying she'd never heard "Mo Ghile Mear" sung "so close to heaven". In Sligo, a man in a fishing cap slipped Tadhg a wink and a bottle of poitín "for emergencies only".

After touring across Ireland and gaining nationwide fame, the Garglers reached a turning point during a sold-out night at Vienna's WUK, the great hall humming under iron beams and old brick—far from the damp snug of the Wren's Nest.

Tadhg stepped forward, letting the hush stretch before he started gargling "She Moved Through the Fair". His voice carried clear and steady. But mid-note, he stopped dead.

A strangled sound caught in his throat, his eyes flaring wide. He clutched at his neck, colour rushing to his face as he staggered back, the song collapsing into silence. Seamus thumped his back. A cough split the quiet, followed by a ragged gasp—then something small and round flew from Tadhg's mouth, skittering across the stage and ricocheting off the woodwork. Once. Twice. The third roll slowed, and the thing came to rest in the spotlight.

A pearl.

Seamus stooped, lifted it carefully, turning it in the light.

Gasping for air, Tadhg rasped, "What in the name of all things holy…?" He snatched the pearl from Seamus's hand and stuffed it into his pocket.

The incident was prominently reported in the *Inis Mór Chronicle* on the Aran Islands.

Pearl Choked Out by Irish Gargler in Vienna.

Fans debated with passion—some proclaimed it a divine gift from the sea, others dismissed it as a freak accident. The local priest called it "a warning", the ferryman swore it was "a blessing", and a pub owner, never one to waste words, said only, "It'll bring trade." The oldest fisherman in Cill na Seacht nIníon sent a letter to the newspaper, claiming, "The sea only gives back what it has marked. He'd best keep it close."

Galway was buzzing. The Garglers were between sets in Tigh Neachtain's on Cross Street, nursing their pints and basking in their success.

"Something's after changing," Siobhan said. "We were grand before, but now? Jaysus, we're somethin' else entirely."

"I'll tell you what's changed." Tadhg pulled the pearl from his pocket. "This beauty. Since Vienna, we've been perfect—thank you, Seamus."

"Aye, well, it's that or they're simply too polite to say we sound like a drownin' choir."

"Ah, will ya stop?" said Siobhan. "It's a bit of shell, not a bleedin' miracle."

Tadhg kissed the pearl. "I'm tellin' ya. This is our lucky charm. We'll never go wrong now."

"Next thing, you'll be sayin' we should start garglin' with holy water."

"Don't be givin' him ideas, Seamus, for the love of God."

The pearl never left Tadhg's side. He carried it everywhere, thumbing it like a lucky stone before each show, and the music never let them down.

But with his new superstition came a new habit. He swapped seawater for whiskey in his jar—not just any whiskey, but the roughest and cheapest. "It gives the tunes warmth," he insisted.

The others tried to intervene. Siobhan, exasperated, snapped, "You can't gargle 'Ode to Joy' pissed, Tadhg!"

"Don't tell me how to gargle."

In Roundstone he proved her right. Mid "Raglan Road", the whiskey scorched his throat; he belched straight through the chorus, dribbling amber down the front of his Aran jumper. The room fell quiet, then a ripple of laughter broke out—not the warm kind that lifted the roof of the Wren's

Nest, but the sharp-edged, mocking sort. Tadhg bowed with a drunken grin, pretending it was part of the act. Siobhan left the stage in silence.

The breaking point came in Cork: drunk, Tadhg stumbled during "The Rocky Road to Dublin" and pitched off the stage. Chairs scraped. Pints were set down. People were gone before the song was done.

One by one, the group disbanded. Padraig followed Siobhan. Even Seamus, loyal to a fault, threw in the towel. "I can't do this anymore—not like this."

Tadhg, stubborn as ever, refused to bend. "I don't need them. I've got this." He patted his pocket where the pearl lay, as if it were the only partner he'd ever trust.

Years later, on a bitter winter's day—it might have been a Thursday—Tadhg, weathered and alone, coat ragged, hands raw, sat hunched on a bench by the River Liffey, the grey water dragging itself past with a thousand tales.

He fumbled in his pocket and found it—smooth, absurdly precious. Old habits returned: he slipped the pearl into his mouth like a lozenge, rolling it across his tongue, tasting memory. A child's trick. A drunk's ritual.

He let it settle in the hollow of his cheek, closed his eyes, and let sleep take him.

The pearl slipped slowly, cutting off his breath. Panic ripped through the haze. He staggered, clutching at his throat, gagging, gasping—until a brutal cough wrenched it free. It landed with a wet thud in his open palm.

He lifted the pearl to the pale winter sun, a hacking cough escaping as he tossed it into the river.

A quiet plop, and it was gone—swallowed by the current, lost for now.

He lifted his flask to his lips; whiskey burned his throat as salt water once had. He tilted his head back and began to gargle—raw, awkward, a low gurgle between croon and choke.

"I've been a wild rover for many a year…"

People stopped. The hum of conversation ebbed. Faces softened, hearing not just the words, but the years braided into them.

The melody rose—the gargle steadying, sweetening, finding tune. "And I spent all me money on whiskey and beer."

The wind carried the last note, thinned to a clear, haunting thread across the Liffey, over the Atlantic, toward the cliffs that had shaped him.

His eyes closed. He smiled, and the song ended with him.

Quiggley Quiggley

Day 14, February 1986 – Valentine's Day

In 1986, South Africa was haemorrhaging. Townships burned, tear gas choked the streets, and the government clung to power like a drunk to a half-empty brandy bottle. And here we were, sent on patrol to make things better—or at least to be seen doing something.

Our Bedford truck rattled up outside a school with no fence and a football pitch worn to dust. We clambered down, rifles slung, boots sinking into the powdered dust. From the low schoolhouse came a man in khaki trousers and a crisp white shirt, walking steadily. He raised a hand in greeting. The sergeant met him with the briefest handshake, then the two moved toward the doorway, the sergeant's shoulders set as if the whole business were an inconvenience.

Paul—our driver and de facto cultural attaché—kick-started the morning with his battered JVC ghetto blaster, stitched together with duct tape, wire, and a strip of tyre tube, its heart clamped to the Bedford's battery. Across his lap, as always, lay his cricket bat—a silent witness from lecture halls to bush patrols, as much a limb as his own arm.

From Paul's playlist of anti-government, anti-establishment, go-fuck-you songs, James Phillips's "Hou My Vas Korporaal" blared out—a glorious middle finger to the powers that be. The platoon endured the jarring tune, humming as the sun bit down.

Paul, Tony, and I were soutpiele, English-speaking South Africans caught between continents; the rest, die-hard Boere. Everyone knew the score. We left their sacred cows alone, and they left ours—mostly. It was a delicate dance, full of unspoken boundaries and half-joked insults.

In the thin strip of shade beneath the Bedford, a one-eyed mongrel sprawled, ribs rising and falling with the weary rhythm of a scavenger. The dog's good eye followed our every move, as if he'd seen enough soldiers to know better than to trust us.

The sergeant re-emerged at last—Sergeant Jakobus Stefanus Koekemoer—his face shadowed with reluctant duty, the headmaster behind him alight with hope. Clearing his throat, Koekemoer forced out, "Men… we haf… new mission. Ja. Important. For… community. This is Mister… Malu… loo… leke—uh—the headmaster." The name snagged in his mouth.

The headmaster stepped forward. "Mister Maluleke," he said gently, correcting him.

The sergeant scratched his neck. "Ja, we go to de dry river. We take sand. We use de spades—for de bricks. Very important. Big job. For de community." The words sagged and collapsed.

Tony broke the silence. "Sarge, are we soldiers or builders now?"

The sergeant's glare said it all. "Builders and soldiers, no jokes. You carry sand for future peoples." His last words hung limp.

The headmaster, beaming, clapped him on the shoulder. "Yes! Your sergeant is a great man!"

The sergeant winced, struggling to keep composure.

Paul raised his bat with a grin. "Sarge looks like he'd rather be anywhere else. His entire bloodline has been insulted."

Tony spat into the dust. "Gatkruip patrollie, bru—brown-nosing patrol. The headmaster's got him by the balls."

We bit back our laughter as the sergeant straightened. "Okay, manne! Get ready. We go now!"

That kicked off the great sand-hauling mission of 1986.

It was bloody hot. Our fatigues were soaked with sweat as we shovelled load after load of sand into the Bedford. Half of the platoon dozed in the shade, snoring like beasts in a pen.

The villagers cheered us on, their eyes bright with amusement and hope. Their cheers rose and fell with the Bedford's engine as it strained beneath every load. Maybe they glimpsed change in our clumsy efforts—or maybe they just relished the absurdity of soldiers reduced to labourers under their sun.

By lunch, the misery was over. Our bodies were coated in sweat and dust. While we tried to recover, Tony announced he was going to see if he could get some beers. I thought of lying down and letting the sun finish me. Eight minutes later,

Tony returned—scuffed tennis ball in one hand, twelve quarts of Black Label (the legendary Zamalek) rattling in a plastic crate carried by a grinning youth.

Tony's smile was pure mischief. "Right, you fuckers," he shouted, "cricket time!"

We rallied as if on a mission—not from God, but from the crate of Zamalek. Beer first, cricket second; the order was clear.

We downed the bottles. When the last was gone, the crate was dragged onto the pitch, serving as a makeshift wicket.

Paul marked out the length of a cricket pitch on the dusty football ground, counting strides aloud—one, two… five… twenty-four—stretching the last step with a grunt before dropping a rock to mark the bowler's crease. At the far end, Tony stood ready, a streak of zinc down his nose like Allan Donald, rolling his shoulders, rubbing the tennis ball on his trousers, practising his run-up.

The noise drew children from doorways and patches of shade until they lined the edge of the field, giggling, whispering, nudging each other. For them, soldiers turning a dust patch into a cricket field must have seemed bizarre, a break from the ordinary, something to remember and retell.

I raised my hand and called them over. They gathered slowly, shy smiles, not knowing what was happening. I kept the rules simple—hit the ball, run between the beer crate at one end and the rock at the other, keep running until the fielders finally got their hands on it and threw it back at the wicket.

Paul and Tony demonstrated the bowling and batting. The children's eyes lit up. Laughter broke out, sharp and contagious. They understood.

The first boy stepped forward, barefoot, no older than ten. I handed him the bat—far too big for his frame. For a moment he just stood there, clutching it awkwardly. Then came the smile, crooked with mischief.

Tony marked out a lazy run. He sent down a slow ball, generous, looping toward the boy. The bat came up stiff and late but struck the ball, sending it skimming through the dust toward the outfield. "Run. Quickly, quickly!" I roared, arms threshing.

The boy kicked up dust as he tore between the wickets, his grin widening with every return. Behind him, fielders piled after the ball, tripping over one another in a storm of elbows and shins. At last, one snatched the ball and charged back, hurling it in a wild arc. It sailed hopelessly past the crate.

The game had begun.

Another crate of beer was delivered to the edge of our makeshift field, the headmaster giving a small, conspiratorial wave that suggested he might be the benefactor.

The next batter stepped up. He smashed the ball. "Quickly, quickly, QUICK-LEE, QUICK-LEE!" I bellowed. Rhythm turned to slur.

Somewhere between the third batter and my fourth bottle of Zamalek, the word slipped, cracked, re-formed in my mouth.

"QUIGGLEY, QUIGGLEY!" I howled. The syllables were mangled beyond recognition. The children at the edge of the field caught it at once, ears sharper than mine, and flung it back. "Quiggley, Quiggley!" they screamed at the runners. The chant was no longer mine, but theirs.

The game spun into delirium. Laughter and cheers met every strike. The crate toppled again and again, rebuilt with ritual patience. At one point, the batter and wicketkeeper charged at once, colliding in a storm of dust and giggles.

The rules dissolved. The game unravelled. Boundaries meant nothing. Stumpings turned into theatre, and the only constant was the chant: "QUIGGLEY, QUIGGLEY!"

Then, with perfect insolence, the music was stolen. The ghetto blaster, once thundering James Phillips and defiance, was hijacked by a village boy who fed it Lucky Dube. "Think About the Children" burst across the field, rhythms folding into the chant, beer flowing freer, the pitch becoming a dance floor.

Amid the chaos, I bowled to Paul, smacked him square on the shins, and bellowed, "Howzat! Ellbeedoubleyouuu," while jabbing a finger skyward in mock umpire style. The kids caught it at once—but gloriously mangled it after watching me. Minutes later, every "Howzat!" turned into a long, drawn-out howl—"Elllbeeeedubbbbleeeyoooo"—arms flung wide, middle fingers brandished in the up-yours fashion, faces lit with mischief.

As the shadows stretched and the sun drowned, the one-eyed mongrel—an inscrutable judge of our lunacy—rose from beneath the truck. With the slow grace of a creature that had seen too much and cared too little, it wandered to our wicket, the beer crate half-buried in dust. It lifted its leg and pissed with unhurried contempt. Without a backward glance, it slipped into the twilight, tail ticking time on the dust.

The day was done. Not cricket by any rules, but it was Quiggley Quiggley—sweat, laughter, rebellion, beer—a reckless afternoon that was enough.

*

A few days after Valentine's Day – 1986

The children greeted us when we returned after Valentine's with grins as wide as the Limpopo River, their voices rising in a jubilant chorus: "Play QUIGGLEY QUIGGLEY!"

They tugged at our hands, pulling us back toward the dusty pitch that had become their sanctuary of joy.

Paul raised the bat. Tony cracked a quart. I shouted. New rules today—no rules!

The sergeant watched from the Bedford. He didn't stop us. Didn't say a word. Just lit a cigarette and looked away.

He was rotated out the next day. No explanation.

We left the village a few days later. As we drove off into the heat, tired and smiling, the kids ran behind us shouting "Quiggley! Quiggley!" until they vanished in the dust.

And so, from a tennis ball, a few quarts of Zamalek, a clash of "Think About the Children" and "Hou My Vas"—and more laughter than sense—the game of Quiggley Quiggley was born.

Back at base, rumours started about a crazy new game being played in the towns. In Dumphries, kids chanted "QUIGGLEY QUIGGLEY!" In Madras, a teacher asked if anyone knew the rules to Quiggley. No one did.

That was the point.

*

Now, years later – Mbombela

Sat in a bar tonight. The barman grinned at me—a crooked, mischievous grin. Poured me a Zamalek, kept one for himself. We chatted.

He remembered a strange game. No rules. Just dust, bare feet, and laughter. He said it was called Quiggley.

"Where did it come from?" I asked.

"No one knows—but I still remember the chant."

I nodded. Kept silent. It was a long time ago.

We weren't heroes. We weren't even good soldiers. One afternoon, in the middle of nowhere, something beautiful happened. A game. A chant. A piss-soaked beer crate. Quiggley Quiggley.

Author's Note:

If anyone ever claims the origin of Quiggley Quiggley, let it be the kids of that village. We were just drunk men with a ball; they made it immortal. As for the name "Quiggley Quiggley"—that's mine. And if it ever finds its way into a dictionary, I'll be waiting with a grin and a crate of Zamalek.

The Boy Who Drank Black Gold *(Akiro Ng'akipi)*

In Turkana, the land speaks to those who listen. The wind whispers through thorn scrub, camels drag their shadows across the horizon, and the dust on the tongue carries its own truth. None listened more closely than Ewoi.

At fourteen, he was wiry, sun-carved, and shaped by Turkana's hunger. Some called him curious; others, cursed. Both names clung to him.

It began on an afternoon when the sky seemed to recoil from the earth's heat.

Ewoi wandered further than he should have, leaving the goats to nose at thorn bushes. A low hum pulled him on—a metallic growl drifting from the Tullow Oil drilling site. Beyond the fences and warning signs, the machines crouched like giant beasts, black-and-yellow hides streaked with dust.

Barefoot on the scorched earth, he crept toward the camp's forgotten edge. There, he found it: the waste oil pit.

A stagnant pool of blackness shimmered in the sun, its skin thick and sluggish. He crouched at the edge, his reflection rippling in the tar-like surface. One finger dipped in—oil clung to it, warm and sticky. He sniffed, then touched it to his tongue. Bitter. Burning. Alive. It crawled down his throat. He coughed, spluttered, wiped his lips… and craved more.

Again his finger dipped, this time scooping deeper. The second taste burned less. The third hinted at sweetness.

Ewoi returned each day with a discarded water bottle, filled it with oil, and drank. Heat surged through him: chest, arms, legs. His teeth clenched, his heart pounded, and he craved more.

One Tuesday morning, when the famine relief trucks rattled into the village, Ewoi slipped away from the noise. He followed the lagga toward the eastern hills, and as midday scorched the land, he left the dry riverbed for shade beneath an acacia thicket.

There he halted, caught by a scent—strange, yet familiar. He crouched, scratched a crooked shape into the dirt, then lowered his head until his nose touched the soil. He breathed, and the fragrance rose through him, carrying the taste of the pit—sharp, sweet, bitter.

Without knowing why, he gathered stones and pebbles, stacking them into a small cairn, an altar in the crooked shape.

Ewoi's cairns, each an echo of the first, soon dotted the scrubland—silent altars whose meaning belonged to him alone.

During a community outreach session, Kiprotich, the Tullow Oil stakeholder engagement officer, caught sight of Ewoi crouched beside one of his cairns, nose pressed to the ground, fingers tracing circles in the dust.

Kiprotich called out, voice sharp. "What are you doing down there?"

Ewoi, with eyes fixed on the ground, lifted the bottle. "There's magic here. See?" His hand twirled the oily bottle.

"Like this. It is akiro ng'akipi—black gold from under the earth."

Kiprotich laughed. "Oil, eh? You can smell it?"

The boy nodded. "It's here." He pointed at the ground with complete certainty, then traced a circle in the dirt with his bottle.

Kiprotich marked the spot in his notebook. Over the next few days, he tested the boy, leading him to random places on the plains. Each time, Ewoi crouched, sniffed, and pointed. "Here," he'd say, tapping the ground. By the third day, Kiprotich's map was dotted with the boy's markers.

At the next briefing, he set down the map. "There's a boy who claims he can sniff oil. Not a joke."

Someone laughed. "What's next? Goats singing the anthem?"

Kiprotich tapped the map. "These are the spots he marked. They match perfectly with our seismic data."

The room fell silent. The operations manager's smirk faded. "You're serious?"

"Yes, sir. As serious as the oil under your feet."

News spread quickly. In Cape Town, the story reached the executive meeting agenda under "Miscellaneous".

"A child sniffing oil? You've got to be kidding me. We pour hundreds of millions into seismic surveys, and you're telling me a barefoot Turkana boy can nose it out like a donkey sniffing a dry riverbed before the rains?"

The Tullow field operations manager, sunburnt, slightly hungover, and road-worn from Turkana, fumbled with the overhead projector. "Gentlemen, you may want to hold your laughter."

The first slide lit the screen: Tullow's seismic map, years of data, millions of dollars of algorithms dressed in colour. A second slide followed—the locations of the boy's cairns laid over the same map.

The room hushed. The points matched perfectly, each circle and cairn echoing the company's invisible riches. A geologist leaned forward, glasses sliding down her nose. The seismic manager tapped his pen once, twice, then stopped.

The operations manager faced them. "Gentlemen, this boy could save you millions."

They set up the rig at the site they named for him—Ewoi-1. The drill bit chewed through rock and sand for nearly a month, day and night, mud pits swirling with cuttings. On the twenty-eighth day, the signs came: sheen on the slurry, a smell sharp as metal, the fluorescence in the samples undeniable. The crew cheered. Ewoi's nose had found oil.

Around the rigs, small towns woke with a restless hunger. Traders sprouted beneath acacia clumps, hawking warm beer, bargain shaving kits, and batteries that disappeared almost as soon as they appeared. Nights crackled with transistor radios and winked with torchlight, and for the first time anyone could remember, men walked home with pockets alive with coins. Soon, people had a name for the thing that had changed their lives. They called it *akiro ng'akipi*—black gold from under the earth.

Outside the manyatta, a pickup rolled to a halt —its side panel stamped with the blue Tullow Oil logo. Men clambered down from the back and began unloading: three goats tugging at their ropes, a sack of tobacco, a bag of sugar. The goats stumbled into the livestock pen, bewildered, their hooves scraping the hard ground. Ewoi's mother knelt by the sack of sugar, running her hands across the coarse fabric as though it were treasure.

A man in a white shirt—flown in from London—cleared his throat. "This, all this, for you. We say thank you… your son… he is great."

Behind him, two pale men in safari hats jostled for the best angle, camera shutters snapping. They grinned at the goats, at the mother bent over the sugar, and at Ewoi's father standing silent in the doorway of the hut.

The family stood mute while the cameras devoured them whole.

Margaret arrived without warning, the Land Cruiser coughing clouds of dry earth as it pulled up at the edge of the manyatta. She stepped down hard, her khaki shirt buttoned to the throat, the Tullow Oil badge stitched sharp above her heart. The goats bleated in their pen, the sack of sugar sat open in the shade like an offering too small to matter.

Ewoi's father hunched beneath an acacia, chewing a stalk of dry grass. Margaret went straight to him.

"Do you know what your son has given them?"

He shifted, startled. "He helps them find the oil. They gave us good things." He gestured vaguely toward the goats, the sack, the tobacco tied with twine.

Margaret's voice hardened. "No. He's not helping. He's making them millions. And this?" She jabbed at the tobacco. "This is what they think he's worth."

Silence thickened. Ewoi shuffled at the edge of the circle, eyes fixed on the horizon, an oily bottle dangling in his hand.

Neighbours had gathered, drawn by the activity, the Land Cruiser, and the sharpness of Margaret's words. Women folded their arms, men leaned on sticks, children peered from behind their mothers' skirts. Margaret rose to face them.

"They use him like a tool. In using him, they insult all of you. Is that enough? Goats and sugar, for your treasure?"

The words lodged. One by one the neighbours nodded, murmuring, their anger a low hum that spread across the plains. In the days that followed, elders and kin sat long under the acacias, voices rising and falling, smoke from their fires curling into the dusk. Decisions hardened at those barazas. By the week's end they no longer spoke of insult, but of action.

At first light they came, a line of bodies rising from the plains like a mirage. Men, women, children—walking barefoot, sticks in hand, scraps of cardboard swinging from twine. The words painted there were crooked but fierce: *Fair Pay for Our Land. Justice for Ewoi.*

Dust lifted around their ankles; chants rolled forward in waves. "Our rights! Our rights! Our oil! Our money!"

A security guard shouted, "They want to talk to the boss—Boss Rob."

Inside the camp, behind tinted glass and humming air conditioners, managers and supervisors pressed their faces to the windows. Their lips barely moved, but their eyes ticked, restless, at the sight of so many. Outside, the rhythm of sticks on tin carried like war drums.

Guards shifted in their boots, hands brushing batons. Rob, the operations manager—half Canadian, half Australian—slouched in his chair, eyes raw from whiskey, voice thick with disdain. "So, they want to talk, do they?" He smirked, then jabbed a finger across the room. "Margaret—go play diplomat, see what song they're singing. And you, Chris—call security, tell them to tighten the cordon. Get the municipal police on standby. If they think we're running a bloody baraza out here, they've picked the wrong field."

Margaret was sent out first. She pushed through the razor-wire gate. Kiprotich trailed behind, wiping sweat from his brow, his clipboard clutched like a shield.

Margaret raised her hands. "We're here to listen! Let us talk!"

The crowd slowed. Elders stepped forward, words tumbling out—land, betrayal, insult, the boy's gift. Margaret argued back in promises, Kiprotich scribbled circles on his pad, children clung to their mothers' legs. For hours the sun hammered down, and something like hope flickered in the heat.

The sound came—a low growl rising over the plain—and heads turned toward the dust climbing the road.

A convoy of police trucks was grinding towards them. They braked hard at the operations gate. Doors flung open and police spilled out, boots thudding against the earth, spreading into a loose formation, rifles hanging at their sides. Rob strolled toward the gate as the police spread into formation, a tin of Coke in his hand. He set the can on the gravel, clapped—slow, deliberate, echoing—and drawled loud enough for all to hear, "It's about fucking time, gentlemen."

The chants faltered, then returned sharper, louder—a roar laced with fear. Someone booed, another spat, and then the jeering spread like fire through dry grass.

Margaret stepped between the police and the community, both hands high. "There's no need for this"

Her words vanished in a crack and hiss. Tear-gas canisters burst, choking white clouds billowing into the crowd. Children screamed, elders staggered, sticks clattered to the dirt. Smoke bombs followed, thunderous, rolling through legs and lungs. Then bullets—the sound of metal ripping air.

People dropped where they stood. Some clutched their legs, others their throats. A woman fell forward still holding her placard, the word *Justice* on the placard beneath her cheek.

Margaret was dragged back by Kiprotich, his face wet with tears or gas, no one could tell.

Behind the fence, managers turned from the windows, their silhouettes blurred in glass. To them, it was an inconvenience, a cost of business.

To the people, it was a betrayal written in blood and smoke that would not fade.

It was not long before the disasters arrived—one after another, relentless as the wind.

The first fire came just before midnight. The rig crew had been dozing in the prefab huts. The alarm sounded, reaching across the plain. Workers ran to their stations.

The derrick was ablaze. Flames clawed up the steel spine, oil-black smoke boiling skyward. Drums popped, sharp as rifle shots. Heat burst their seams. A mechanic tried to run for the water truck. Too late. The hoses were split, ends gaping like dry mouths. The foreman screamed orders no one could hear. The roar drowned everything else.

By dawn, all that remained was a skeletal frame, glowing red at the joints.

Over the following weeks, one rig after another erupted into flames, their remains glowing orange against the night sky. Workers fled in terror, abandoning tools and machinery to rust in the desert wind. Water trucks never arrived. Food ran out. Bandits took to the roads.

Ewoi walked the plains alone, nose twitching to scents no one else could name. The land was quiet now.

He climbed the ridge at dusk. On the summit: a cairn, taller than him, leaning toward the setting sun. Below, the rigs lay broken. Their steel spines were sinking into the earth. One well still smoked—grey incense rising into the darkening sky.

He crouched at the cairn, one hand touching the stone, and closed his eyes. It was there—not only earth and stone, but something older, deeper, pulsing through the rock.

And the boy, anointed by its depths, was the only one it answered.

The Unwilling Import

The SS *Verwoerd's* funnels chugged black smoke into Durban's skyline as it sailed out of port. Bound for Canada, its decks were stacked with containers of tribal masks, carved giraffes, and counterfeit relics—cargo fated for garage sales and customs oblivion. But among the crates was one that should never have left the shore.

Across the Atlantic, six hundred nautical miles west of the Azores, a storm pummelled the ship. Waves battered the hull, ropes snapped, and crates vanished. Yet one dog kennel–sized box broke loose and drifted on, carried by the current until it washed ashore at Trá Leitreach Cove, near Inis Meáin three weeks later.

Cian O'Malley spotted the crate during his morning sweep of the beach—a ritual stroll he liked to call "treasure-hunting".

"What've we got here?"

He pulled a crowbar from his rucksack. The nails shrieked as he prised open the lid. Inside were masks, beaded necklaces, carved figurines—souvenirs tourists went mad for. He started dreaming up prices, already calculating how much a "rare Bantu fertility totem" might fetch. But then something else grabbed his attention.

At the bottom of the crate, nestled in straw, lay a stone—blacker than the Devil's gallstone, he thought. Warm in his palm, heavier than it ought to be, its surface was etched with faint spirals that hinted at script, or maybe a map. His gut whispered to hurl it back into the tide. But Cian O'Malley was not in the habit of throwing away potential profit. He slipped the stone into his backpack, added a few smaller trinkets, and shut the lid on the rest. Tearing a scrap from his notebook, he scrawled a note and nailed it to the crate:

Mine. Don't touch. Will collect later. Signed O'Malley—yes, that O'Malley.

Shouldering the bag, he left the beach and trudged up the lane to O'Malley's Curios and Treasures in the heart of Inis Meáin village.

He unpacked his haul. Masks were propped between lobster traps and maritime trinkets. Necklaces dangled from a rusted ship's bell. The black stone he placed on a shelf beside a broken sextant and a one-eyed doll that had unnerved children for years. It looked quite at home, he thought.

Eleven days later, as the black stone settled into its new home, strange goings-on unsettled the islanders of Inis Meáin. The air thickened with the stench of rotting seaweed. Milk soured overnight, bread bloomed mould before dawn, and dogs balked at passing O'Malley's Curios and Treasures. The postman swore he saw shadows moving inside, though the shop was locked. Then came the noises—low, guttural chuckles that slithered through the lanes at ungodly hours. The signs darkened swiftly. A fisherman's net was found shredded, though no storm had passed. In his field, a farmer discovered his prized ram lying stiff, the body unmarked, the eyes frozen wide with terror. And Brigid O'Donnell swore she glimpsed a small, shadowed figure flitting through her garden at dusk.

By week's end, the tales had gathered where they always did—in the Crooked Shillelagh, the pub nailed to the cliff above Inis Meáin village. There, gossip thickened into certainty. A woman spoke of hoofprints pressed into the soil near her barn, the ground blackened and brittle. Another swore her doors had rattled in the still of night, tools in her shed shifted from their hooks. Each voice added a fragment, and by the time the whiskey had circled twice, Mairead declared, "It's the pooka, for sure. The trickster spirit has come back to torment us."

In the corner sat Fred Lammergeier with a pint of Guinness—his fourth, maybe fifth. He'd come all the way from Durban for the Aran Literary Festival, a modest gathering, to talk about his book, *Spirits of the Zulu Kingdom*. Years of chasing folklore had convinced him every tale carried at least a grain of truth. But tonight, the pub talk was far more entertaining.

Fred lifted his glass, wiped the foam from his moustache with the back of his hand, and with perfect timing said, "In South Africa, we call Guinness 'Mandela'." He paused, tapped the rim. "You get it? Black… with a white head."

A beat later, laughter rippled through the Crooked Shillelagh. Even Pádraig Ó Riain, sceptical of anything foreign, let out a chuckle.

Fred set down his pint. "This isn't a pooka... This"—he tapped the table—"is an uthikoloshe."

Cian squinted. "An ooh-ti-what-now?"

Fred rolled the name slowly. "An uthikoloshe."

"A... oo... thik... a-losh...?"

"No, no, not quite. You can't roll it off the tongue, can you?"

Paudie said, "Ah, I can't even get past the first part! What are ye sayin' there, man?"

"You lot would just call it tokoloshe, like every other white person who can't get their tongue around it."

"Wait, wait—who are ye, and what's this... ah, tokoloshe thing?"

"I'm Nqobizitha Lammergeier. From Tekweni, South Africa."

The room fell silent, everyone trying to wrap their heads around the name.

"Say that again?"

"I said Nqobizitha Lammergeier—Nqo-bi-zee-ta. My old journalism tutor drilled phonetics into us: break it down, make it sing on the tongue... innnn-khhhohh-bee-zee-tahhhh."

"I can't even say that in my sleep..."

Fred shook his head, amused. "Look, just call me Fred. No one ever gets it right." He took another sip of Guinness. "I came for the Aran Literary Festival to discuss my book, *Spirits of the Zulu Kingdom*."

"Fred, eh? I can do Fred." Cian raised his pint, nodding. "Cheers to Fred. Now tell us about this talkallosssheeee."

"It's not just mischievous, it's malevolent. Back home, people fear it the way you fear drought or hunger. The pooka might topple a haystack or hide your keys, but the tokoloshe… it suffocates you in your sleep, poisons your food, and doesn't stop there. It thrives on fear."

A voice called out, "What does it look like, this tokorlosheeee?"

"It changes. Sometimes it's small and hunched, more bone than skin. Other times it's tall and bent, like a man broken in two who still keeps moving. The worst part… they've no eyes. But they see you just fine." Fred swirled his Guinness, taking his time. "And here's the cruel bit—some never see it at all. Others see it plain as day. If it chooses you, that's it. Once it does, you're finished."

He let that sit for a moment, taking another slow sip.

"That's why back home we raise our beds on bricks. Because if you don't"—he paused, letting the tension build—"you wake up in the middle of the night and it's already squatting on your chest, pressing the air out of your lungs. You try to scream, but no sound comes out. You fight, but there's nothing to grab onto. The only thing you feel is its hands tightening around your throat."

A log split in the fire.

Fred let the silence stretch. "No bricks… and you'll feel it crushing your chest before you even open your eyes."

Silence followed. Then the muttering began—a hissed "Mother a' God", a chair scraping, someone cursing they'd not sleep a wink that night. From the back came a laugh, but it died fast when no one joined in.

Pádraig Ó Riain scratched his beard and cut across them. "So, you're saying it's not the pooka at all?"

Fred shook his head firmly. "Not the pooka. The pooka tricks, unsettles, maybe frightens. But this…" He tapped the table. "This kills."

Cian and the villagers weighed Fred's words. Someone muttered about old stories in Clare, another about cattle gone missing in Mayo. Slowly, as pints lifted and heads nodded, Cian felt the island's certainty shift—whether they believed Fred or just liked a new name for it, the tokoloshe had replaced the pooka in their minds.

"So," Cian said, "what do we do?"

Fred drained the last of his pint, set the glass down with a clunk, and burped. "Salt! Salt everywhere, iron in every corner, and bricks under your beds. I don't care if you've never done it before. You will tonight."

From the back came a shout: "No bricks here, only shitloads of limestone blocks."

Fred shrugged. "Then use limestone. It'll work. Shitloads of it. The uthikoloshe feeds on fear. Show weakness and it will know. Falter, and it comes for you. So whatever prayers you've got, say them. And for God's sake—" He slammed the glass down. "Raise your beds!"

He put his hand to his mouth to cover a burp. "Oh. What's the name of that church? The one near the cliff?"

The crowd in the pub answered in unison, "Saint Eoin's!"

From the corner of the pub, Father Seamus, sitting in his favourite chair, cleared his throat. "For the record, it's Séipéal Eoin agus Naomh Muire gan Smál. Or, if that's too much for ye lot, the Church of Saint John and the Immaculate Mary."

"Fine, whatever. Meet me at St John's tomorrow night. Midnight. What you lot have been jabbering about—dead sheep, nets torn to shreds—that's not random, it's a warning. Means the bastard's closing in. So here's what you do. Bring salt—bags of it, barrels if you've got them. Bring iron—nails, horseshoes, bloody anchor chains if that's all you can find. Salt stings it, iron wounds it, and the more of it you've got, the better your chances of keeping your throats intact. And don't forget your prayers. Any old nonsense will do, Hail Marys or half-remembered hymns, just keep the noise up.

"And for God's sake—" He slammed his glass on the table again. "Raise your beds!"

At first light, Fred's words had the island in a frenzy. Men ripped walls apart, women dug up gardens, neighbours shouted back and forth as limestone blocks were dragged and stacked in heaps.

By sundown, every bed on Inis Meáin stood perched on stone, swaying and uneasy, a fortress against whatever was coming.

By the twelfth peal of the church bell, the village had crammed into St Eoin's, clutching sacks of salt and jagged iron scraps like peasants braced for a medieval exorcism. The church hunched grimly on the cliff-edge, leaning into the Atlantic. Wind screamed through the stone, rattled the shutters, shoved its way through every crack in its frame.

At the altar stood Fred, waving his arms and shouting orders like a man possessed. His voice bounced off the stone walls, a mix of rage and absurdity. "It attacks on nights like this. Get salt on the windowsills. Iron in the corners. Move! And pray, damn it—anything you know! I don't care what it is, just keep it loud!"

They poured salt in wide, jagged lines. Soon, the church floor resembled the fever dream of a psychotic pastry chef. They piled and hammered rusted horseshoes, bent nails, and rusty boat anchors into every corner and nook of the church. And then the chanting started—a chaotic symphony of mangled Latin, Irish ballads, and a rendition of "Shoulder to Shoulder".

Father Seamus lurched up to the altar, a tattered Bible in one hand and a half-empty bottle of Paddy in the other, looking like a man set to wrestle saints and demons alike. He uncapped the whiskey with priestly solemnity, raised it like the chalice, and took a long swig before passing it to Fred. Fred downed a quarter and tucked the bottle into his jacket.

"Libera nos a malo, Domine!" Father Seamus thundered. "Deliver us from evil, O Lord!"

The villagers froze, then stumbled into the chant, their voices ragged but rising in frantic unity.

"Ní féidir leis an dorchadas an solas seo a ghabháil!" he cried. "The darkness cannot claim this light!"

And then the final plea, a bellow to the patron saint of the cliffs. "Sanctus Eoin, ár garda farraige, cosain muid ón diabhal atá ag teacht! Saint Eoin, our guardian of the sea, protect us from the Devil that approaches!"

The chanting rose—a clash of Latin, Irish, and panic. Someone even claimed to hear a Zulu war cry in the mix. The church shuddered as the storm pressed in.

Candles guttered. Shadows writhed on the walls, clawing at the salt lines. The villagers huddled closer as the timbers groaned like something straining to get in.

Fred strode among them, straightening salt, barking at gaps, bellowing over the din. "Focus! This thing feeds on fear. If you falter, it will know." The words hit like a slap, and the villagers, terrified but stubborn, drove their voices higher in ragged defiance.

Back at Cian's shop, the black stone, nestled between the one-eyed doll and the broken sextant, glimmered faintly in the dark.

"Raise it!" Fred roared, arms wide. "Raise your voices or be damned!"

And they did. Psalms collided with ballads, curses were shouted as prayers, and nonsense syllables rang with pleading. One man bellowed the names of his dead sons; a woman shrieked in a trance, jerking like a puppet.

The gale howled. Air pressed heavy on their chests. Some dropped to their knees, gasping, sure that hands were throttling them. Others swore they saw it—crouched in the rafters, crawling the walls, leering at the windows. No two visions agreed. Still, the frenzy grew. Shadows thickened. Doors rattled. Shutters slammed in their frames.

Fred's voice cut through the shrieking chaos. "Louder! Don't let it feed! Drive it back—drive it back! IT IS HERE!"

Thunder exploded overhead, the windows bulged inward, and a chorus of terror and defiance filled the church, raw and desperate.

The villagers unleashed their final defence, screaming as they hurled anvils, rusted traps, shears, wheelbarrows, and sacks of salt like weapons at the churning shadows—iron raining down, salt blazing across the ground, metal banging furiously as the evil battered the doors. Blood pounded in every ear; hope frayed, but they pressed on, a wall of human noise thrumming with desperate power.

Suddenly, the wind plummeted. Candles steadied. The church trembled once more, then grew eerily silent.

The villagers sagged into pews, panting, their skin slick with sweat, eyes wide and hollow.

At the altar, Fred slowly raised his arms, eyes shining with a mix of triumph and madness. "It's gone," he declared, as if he'd driven off the Devil himself.

By dawn, they stumbled out into the grey light, spent and shaken. Whatever had happened in the night, they believed that Fred's plan—mad as it was—had saved them.

Three days later, as Fred hauled luggage to the ferry for Rossaveel, Cian watched an American tourist pause at that same shelf in his shop. The stranger's fingers drifted over the black stone. Cian's inner hustler awoke—slick words, a shrewd price, and the stone was soon wrapped and sold. That night, it started its journey to Manhattan. Cian locked up, weighed by a feeling he couldn't name.

Fred's own journey veered south—Johannesburg, Flight 417. He relaxed into his seat, sipping a glass of Paddy whiskey.

A stewardess passed by, and Fred flashed her a smile, lifting his glass in a silent request for another round. His notebook, crammed with half-legible scribbles, sat on his lap. Between sketches and cryptic notes, phrases like "Guinness for bravery" and "Never discount limestone—or salt and iron" marked the margins. The Inis Meáin episode stoked his creative fire.

A week later, Johannesburg heat humming through the window slats, Fred sat opposite his publisher in a café off

Commissioner Street. The table was sticky, the fan barely turning.

"So," the publisher said, stirring sugar into his coffee, "what's next, Fred? You disappeared to some island and came back looking like you've seen a ghost."

Fred grinned. "Maybe I did. I'm calling it *Shadows Over the Cliffs*. Irish storm meets African bones. Folklore on both sides of the sea."

The publisher raised an eyebrow. "Ghost stories sell if there's truth in them. You sure it's finished?"

"Not finished," Fred said. "Just begun. The story's still moving. These things migrate, you know. They don't die. They just cross borders."

Across the ocean, in a Manhattan apartment full of traffic hum and half-drawn blinds, the black stone sat on a mantel. The light from a neon sign blinked against its surface. A faint pulse shimmered in the grain.

And far away again, on Inis Meáin, beds still stood on limestone blocks. The villagers said it was only for tradition now, though they never slept easy when the wind turned from the west. Tourists took photographs, laughed, and moved on.

Fred drained the last of his coffee. "It's all connected," he said. "Ireland, Africa, anywhere people still whisper to the dark."

The publisher smiled, thinking he meant folklore. But Fred was staring past him, past the window glass, at something only he could feel—the faint, familiar shift of a story finding its next home.

The Blue Ribbon

It was the night before the Flemish Giant Rabbit Show Championship. The Belgian village of Sint-Amelberga hummed with expectation. The River Dender wound through the fields like liquid pewter, reflecting the hazy moonlight.

Albert Claes, the reigning champion, lounged in the tavern De Slapende Haas ("The Sleeping Hare"), swirling his glass of Duvel and soaking in the glow of his own confidence. Magnus, his rabbit, was a colossus—every inch perfectly sculpted, his fur gleaming like moonlit metal. Victory felt as certain as sunrise.

Behind the bar, Marianne Gils, the petite and striking proprietress, poured drinks with practised grace, her laughter ringing out as she bantered with the regulars. Her smile hid not only the sting of five consecutive defeats at Albert's hands, but a growing resolve to finally dethrone him and restore her family's pride.

This year felt charged for Marianne. She had Louise.

The first whisper of Louise's name started at De Slapende Haas, passing between pints of Duvel and plates of lukewarm fries. By morning, it had slipped into the baker's shop, where women clutching loaves of crusty bread spoke of Louise's noble lineage with the reverence usually reserved for saints. By midday, it was being debated over espressos in the cafés, dissected in front rooms cluttered with knitting and half-eaten waffles, and by evening, it had travelled the full circuit of the village—swelling, twisting, expanding like dough left to rise too long.

By the time the rumour reached the village's most eccentric souls, it had shed all doubt and blossomed into gospel truth.

Louise was no ordinary rabbit.

They said her bloodline was so pure her ancestors dined on heirloom carrots in the kitchen gardens of the Habsburgs' palaces. Others insisted she descended from a Flemish duke's cherished pets, painted alongside his children.

After more retellings in De Slapende Haas, the stakes rose: Louise's lineage now traced to a lost medieval manuscript, where monks described a rabbit so magnificent they believed it an emissary of heaven.

Her great-great-grandfather, Baron van Snuffel III, had once been weighed on a butcher's scale; judges refused to believe a rabbit could tip past eighteen kilogrammes. Louise's mother, Celestine of the Velvet Paw, had starred in the infamous Flemish Fur Scandal of 2014, when an illegal fur-conditioning serum led to her disqualification.

Of course, the great unanswered question remained, puzzling even the faithful. If her lineage was recorded—painted, weighed, scandalised, sainted—why did Louise herself appear nowhere in the studbooks? No photograph, no certificate, no official trace.

Breeders gossiped, speculating about Louise's size, stance, and the sheen of her fur. At the baker's, whispers grew that she was twice the size of the reigning champion, Magnus. At the café, her whiskers were said to curl perfectly. Some believed Marianne herself had sparked the rumour, purposefully dropping Louise's name in conversation and then stepping back to watch the village react. Others swore Marianne was calmly outmanoeuvring everyone, waiting for the exact moment to unveil Louise—keeping even the judges guessing until the last possible second.

Marianne watched the village's excitement build, her patience unwavering.

Some villagers began to wonder if Louise was real at all, since not a single soul in Sint-Amelberga had ever laid eyes on her.

Marianne had made certain of that.

The door of De Slapende Haas creaked open, ushering in a gust of cool evening air. A man stepped inside. He was tall and thin, his face pale, nose sharp, and cheekbones carved like ice. The brim of his hat hung low.

He walked straight to Albert's table.

The man sat down opposite Albert uninvited, folding his coat as he settled into the chair. Albert looked up, frowning, his fingers tightening around his beer glass.

"You're the breeder?" The man's accent was foreign to Sint-Amelberga—Dutch? French? Something else entirely, from no village Albert could name.

"That's right. What's it to you?"

The man smiled, his teeth sharp and whiter than snow. "They say Magnus is perfection. A marvel of symmetry."

Albert's frown eased at the compliment. "They'd be right."

The man tilted his head. "And yet… doesn't perfection feel a bit dull? Predictable?"

"Perfection wins ribbons."

The man chuckled. "Ah, yes. Ribbons. But true greatness doesn't come from following the rules. It comes from breaking them."

Albert shifted in his seat, the lively pub dissolving into a distant, dreamlike haze. "Magnus is perfect as he is."

The stranger's smile widened, his words sliding like honey. "Perfection may win ribbons, but a masterpiece… That changes everything. Imagine Magnus not as a rabbit but as an expression—a challenge to the old ways, something immortalised in memory, not just in trophies."

Albert stared at him, the words swirling in his head. The glass felt heavier in his hand.

"A statement," he repeated, the idea taking hold.

Marianne polished beer glasses, eyes narrowed in concentration as she tracked the exchange between Albert and the stranger, weighing every gesture and word, her lips pressed into a faint, knowing smile.

The stranger sprang to his feet, his coat brushing against the table. "Be bold, Albert. Make Magnus unforgettable."

Before Albert could respond, the stranger tipped his hat and walked out into the night.

Albert drained the last of his beer and walked home, the stranger's words echoing in his mind, stirring something restless within him. "Make Magnus unforgettable."

Back in his barn, Albert stood before Magnus's pen, his chest tight. Magnus blinked at him, calm and unaware of his owner's turmoil.

"You're not just a rabbit. You're a canvas."

He grabbed the scissors.

The first snip sent a pale tuft of fur spiralling to the floor. Albert worked with wild urgency, sculpting jagged ridges into Magnus's coat, his hands racing as inspiration seized him.

Then came the dye.

Broad strokes of crimson and ultramarine streaked Magnus's fur, mingling with soft ochre and deep black. Albert's hands moved with a strange, frenzied precision, the colours swirling like a Nicolas de Staël painting.

Albert staggered back, breathless. Magnus sat utterly still, transformed into a living canvas—his fur a wild eruption of colour and texture, a masterpiece shattered and reassembled anew.

Albert nodded, his lips curling into a smile. "Magnificent."

*

Sunlight streamed onto rows of gleaming tables where breeders displayed their prized rabbits, each cage shrouded in deep-blue cloth. Outside, the aroma of waffles and roasted chestnuts drifted from food carts.

The hall hushed as the judges entered, grizzled men in tweed with creased brows and notable moustaches—each moustache an emblem of authority, from Judge Van Geel's twirl to Judge De Meyer's legendary handlebar.

Clipboards in hand, they moved with the rhythm of men who took their duties seriously. Judge De Meyer cleared his throat—a deep, rasping sound, like a man about to deliver a verdict of national importance. Judge Van Geel adjusted his spectacles and scrutinised a detailed checklist.

✓ Ear symmetry

✓ Weight-to-body ratio

✓ Gloss factor of fur (minimum 8.5 on the Belgian Shine Scale™)

✓ Foot floof density

✓ General aura of nobility

Koenraad Verschueren, the youngest and most nervous of the judges, scribbled wildly, desperate to prove himself. He squeezed in between his elders, muttering observations with the grave intensity of a man inspecting the crown jewels.

One by one, the blue cloths were lifted.

Gasps fluttered through the hall as each rabbit emerged—pristine, glossy-furred champions poised like living sculptures in their cages. A woman in the front row clutched her pearls. A child piped up, "Papa, is that one a prince?" An elderly breeder dabbed at a tear, undone by the breathtaking beauty on display.

The judges nodded gravely, muttering as they stroked their moustaches.

"Zeer indrukwekkend. Note the posture—very confident."

"A fine nose-to-tail ratio. Quite exquisite."

"The sheen, oh, the sheen—it is like polished mahogany!"

Then came Magnus's turn.

Judge De Meyer hesitated, his hand hovering above the cloth. The crowd hushed. A woman at the back stood on her tiptoes. A man near the refreshments dropped his waffle, too enraptured to notice.

The cloth was pulled away.

Silence.

A single fork clattered onto a plate in the distance. A child farted.

Magnus was a spectacle. His once flawless fur was now an explosion of colour, a chaotic masterpiece of crimson, ultramarine, and jagged streaks of ochre and black. His shaved ridges gave him a sculpted, cubist quality—if Picasso had ever turned his hand to rabbits.

A woman in the front row gasped as though witnessing a scandalous affair. An elderly man clutched his chest, muttering, "Mon Dieu." A small child burst into uncontrollable giggles, pointing at Magnus with youth's innocent, brutal honesty.

Judge Van Geel's spectacles slid down his nose. Judge De Meyer's moustache quivered in silent alarm. Koenraad Verschueren just stared, his pen frozen above his clipboard.

Albert stood beside the cage, chest puffed out, triumphant.

Marianne stood near the judges' table, her white-furred Louise radiant under the morning light. Marianne's emotions flickered from disbelief to utter delight as her eyes darted between Magnus and Albert.

"Magnus isn't just a rabbit," Albert declared to the stunned judges, his voice swelling with conviction. "He's an expression. A reflection of modern times!"

The head judge, his face an unreadable mask, finally exhaled. He rubbed his chin. "Schitterend…"

"But—this is highly unusual."

Albert's grin widened. "Unusual is the future!"

A ripple of hushed Flemish debate erupted between the judges.

"It is… avant-garde."

"It is offensive."

"It is… possibly genius?"

"It is undeniably… a rabbit."

As the judges spoke, Albert's clarity returned—doubt struck hard.

He stared at Magnus, and the colours and shapes became grotesque in the frosty morning light.

Albert's triumphant posture wilted. His fingers tightened around the edge of Magnus's cage. "What… what have I done?"

The blue ribbon went to Marianne Gils, who accepted it with a modest smile.

At the back of the crowd, the stranger in the long coat watched with muted satisfaction.

That evening, as the last rays of sunlight shimmered on the River Dender, Marianne stood on the stone bridge. The stranger approached, his coat billowing in the breeze.

She handed him a small pouch of coins. "You promised me the ribbon."

"And you have it." He tipped his hat and turned, walking away without another word.

At Hof Claes, Albert's smallholding on the village's edge, Magnus now roamed between the house, the barn, and the open fields, never to be shown again. His offspring surrounded him, their fur soft and untainted by dye.

Inside the barn-turned-studio, Albert stood before an easel, his hands streaked with paint. The walls were covered with canvases—bold, jagged creations in red, yellow, and blue. He worked on his next abstract painting with feverish intensity, his brush moving in chaotic, determined strokes.

Watching through the open barn door, Magnus twitched an ear and hopped into the field.

The Cut-Up Conduit

The auction house was no Sotheby's. Yellowed posters clung to the rafters; warped floorboards sagged under years of weight. The place was faded, a little jaded. Perfect for tonight's sale.

Collectors, dreamers, scavengers filled the hall, each hunting scraps of genius to claim. Tonight, William S. Burroughs lured them in. Not the man—long dead, still smoking in the afterlife—but his pen and notebook, artifacts heavy with legend.

The Parker 51 sat in its case. It commanded attention like a blade catching light. Its black body was worn smooth where fingers had gripped it, the silver cap dulled to a tired glow. But the nib—fine, sharp, steel—still gleamed under the yellow bulbs. Built for precision. For permanence.

The auctioneer, a thin man with spectacles balanced on his nose, adjusted his tie and tapped the glass as if daring the pen to react.

"Ladies and gentlemen," he began, "this is no ordinary pen. This is the Parker 51, a marvel of engineering. Released in 1941, it was called 'the pen of the century' for good reason. Sleek. Modern. Timeless. Its hooded nib was revolutionary—it doesn't dry out, leak, or fail."

He paused.

"But this Parker 51 is more. It was William S. Burroughs's pen. He carried it everywhere. Some say he drafted his last letters with it; others claim he wrote parts of *The Western Lands* with it and used it in his cut-up experiments. And some"—his voice dipped—"believe Burroughs thought writing could channel something else. That this pen wasn't just a tool, but a conduit."

Beside it lay the notebook: cracked leather cover, dark as bruised skin, fragile yet defiant.

"And this notebook," the auctioneer said softly, "is where things become even more intriguing."

He eased it open with a gloved hand, careful, as though it might crumble to dust. Yellowed, warped pages peeked from the edges.

"The contents are... fascinating. Chaotic, yes, but fascinating. Many pages feature Burroughs's infamous cut-up technique, where sentences are sliced apart, shuffled, and reassembled into strange, prophetic fragments. On one page, for instance"—he squinted at the ink—"'The word eats the man, and the man feeds the word.' Classic Burroughs."

He flipped a few pages. The creak of the spine was soft, but audible. "But there's more. Sketches. Faces drawn with shaking hands—half familiar, half nightmarish. Notes scribbled in the margins: recurring phrases, cryptic symbols. And here..." He stopped, and when he spoke again his voice was slightly lower. "Here are fragments of what appears to be an unpublished novel. A novel Burroughs never spoke of, never shared. Sentences unfinished. Ideas hanging in the air like ghosts."

Several bidders were present, but three stood out as determined buyers.

Closest to the auctioneer sat Lydia Marlowe. She'd spent decades excavating writers' lives, clawing at fragments of genius. Hemingway's letters. Dickinson's scribbles. Always near enough to touch greatness but never possess it.

The auctioneer returned to the Parker 51. "And who knows…? The ink left in this pen"—he paused, glancing at the crowd with the faintest smile—"could very well be the same ink used on these pages."

It was a ridiculous suggestion—ink dries, pens are refilled—but Lydia felt a shiver climb her spine.

Two rows behind sat Phil, gaunt and restless, fingers drumming. Phil didn't crave literary glory. He was a dealer, a middleman for the eccentric wealthy. His client, a Silicon Valley mogul, collected the strange. The man's order: "The pen. Get me the pen."

Near the back, in half-light, sat a young man in frayed jeans and a faded hoodie, out of place among shining shoes and watches. His unkempt hair shadowed his eyes.

"Ladies and gentlemen," the auctioneer intoned, "we'll begin with the Parker 51 pen. Starting at ten thousand pounds."

Lydia's paddle rocketed up. "Fifteen."

Phil leaned back in his chair. "Thirty."

The young man tilted his head. "Fifty."

The auctioneer blinked, taken aback, but recovered swiftly. "Fifty thousand. Do I hear sixty?"

Lydia's pulse quickened. She hadn't expected the price to rise so rapidly. Still, she'd come prepared. "Sixty."

Phil scratched his chin, annoyed. "Eighty."

"One hundred!" from the young man.

The crowd stirred. A hundred thousand pounds… for a pen?

"One hundred thousand. Going once… Going twice…"

Lydia tightened her grip on the paddle. The notebook mattered to her. Let the pen go.

"Sold." The gavel struck.

The young man didn't smile. He watched the Parker 51 vanish offstage.

The auctioneer's voice dipped lower. "And now, the notebook. Burroughs's final thoughts. Unfiltered. Starting at twenty thousand pounds."

Lydia's paddle shot up. "Twenty-one."

Phil followed quickly. "Thirty."

"Fifty."

Phil hesitated. "Seventy."

The young man cleared his throat. "One hundred."

Lydia's knuckles whitened around her paddle. "One-twenty."

Phil let out a low curse. He was done.

The auctioneer addressed the back of the room. "One-twenty to the lady. Do I hear one-fifty?"

"Three hundred."

Lydia turned slowly toward the back of the room. He hadn't moved. Still seated, face half-obscured by shadow, hands folded neatly in his lap.

The auctioneer cleared his throat. "Three hundred thousand. Going once… Going twice… Sold."

The gavel fell. The young man collected the pen and notebook and slipped out the side door. Lydia followed. Phil trailed close behind.

They found him under the streetlamp. Its light faltered, casting him in and out of shadow. In his hand, the Parker 51 gleamed, held like something sacred.

Then he snapped it clean in two.

The pieces slipped through the sewer grate. Gone.

Lydia lurched forward. "What the hell are you doing?"

He didn't answer. He opened the notebook, tearing out page after page. The scraps lifted, caught in the air, and floated into the night.

His outline began to blur. As Lydia stared in shock, what she saw defied explanation. His body dissolved into shifting words and letters. His hands became broken sentences. He was nothing but fragments—drifting up, scattering into the air. It was as if the man, and whatever force possessed him, was written out of existence. Only scraps were left behind.

At dawn, a scavenger shuffled past the bins. Something caught his eye—a single page, edges curled, ink sharp in the light. He picked it up, straining to read the words.

The pen moves, but only where it's told. The ink doesn't lie.

He frowned, shoved it back into the rubbish, and moved on.

Carbon Copy

Rain turned Camden into a blur of light and puddles. Posters sagged from lampposts, their ink bleeding into the wet. Boniface kept his head down, sensing the city's heaviness, drizzle soaking his coat as the sky pressed against the rooftops.

Boniface was twenty-three, easily overlooked. He haunted Camden libraries, half-empty pubs, night buses. His shoulder bag bulged with notebooks, leaking pens, and scraps of poetry no one wanted to read, yet he wrote because he couldn't help it.

Tonight, though, there was something in the air. A change. Rain echoed it against shop windows, and Boniface's feet, soaked in threadbare boots, led him somewhere unexpected: Gideon & Finch, a curiosity shop wedged between a vape shop and a tattoo parlour.

The door groaned. Inside was a cave of forgotten things. Light seeped through grime. Books with crumbling spines slumped on shelves, figurines stared from cabinets, portraits—faces faded—peered down at him.

The air scratched his throat—wax polish over damp. A clock ticked in the back. Carefully, Boniface avoided brushing anything, half-afraid the shop might collapse at a touch.

And then he saw it.

The Underwood No. 5. Black enamel dulled but intact. The platen straight, the carriage firm, the keys worn smooth from years of hammering…

"Beautiful, ain't she?" a voice hissed from behind.

Turning, he saw the proprietor: a thin man with sagging shoulders, yellowing eyes, and teeth like cracked porcelain.

"Works a treat," he said, tapping the glass with a pale, stained fingernail. "They say it belonged to someone proper famous. You know Plath?"

"Plath?" Boniface questioned.

"The poet. The one that stuck her head in the gas oven. No proof, mind. Just talk. But a good story don't need the truth, does it?"

"How much?"

"Fifty quid. Fair price for a legend."

Boniface walked home—the rain coming down, the typewriter wrapped in newspaper and tucked into an old Tesco shopping bag.

Back in his freezing bedsit above the incense shop and the kebab joint he set the Underwood on his desk.

He sat at the typewriter. It waited, dark and patient. Beside it, a chipped mug of chamomile steamed. The radiator clattered.

He fed a sheet into the rollers, turning the platen until the paper curled into place. The carriage groaned. Boniface flexed his fingers, exhaled, and began to type.

The first lines stammered out—awkward, gasping, fragmented, just as he liked them…

city-night beats / streetlights / blinking tired / eyelids of stone…

Words shattered, clashed, ee cummings Boniface's secret muse.

For hours, he typed. Fingers hammered the keys. The clack-clack echoed until the radiator stilled and the tea went cold. Pages churned out—jarring rhythms and fractured stanzas only Boniface could cherish.

By dawn, the pages were stacked. Boniface slid them into a battered shoebox under his desk with dozens of others—poems existing only as clatter and ink. He needed the Underwood: the keys' resistance, rhythm, the machine's voice shaping his own.

He knew the world didn't care for clatter.

Later that day, he hunched over his laptop, retyping each piece line for line, translating the weight of paper into the weightlessness of pixels.

Boniface spent the next day polishing his best work, typing out letters to every literary journal he could think of.

Dear Editor, please find attached my poems. I hope they resonate. Sincerely, Boniface Turner.

He clicked send.

At first, Boniface checked his email every five minutes, then every hour. Hours turned into days, and then, after two weeks, the rejections began.

Thank you for your submission. Unfortunately, this isn't a fit for us at this time.

Derivative.

Lacks originality.

Boniface slumped at his desk, the rejection emails dragging him down, doubt gnawing at what little confidence he had.

He woke to a rap at his door. It was his neighbour. "That bloody typewriter clacking at three a.m. again?"

Boniface flushed. "I… write."

The man snorted. "Well, stop it. Bloody racket."

The door slammed. The sound reverberated through Boniface's chest.

That night, he lay in bed, knees pulled close, staring at the Underwood's dark shape. The streetlamp cast a thin ribbon of gold across its enamel frame.

His eyelids sagged. The cold dragged him into a restless half-sleep.

And then something strange happened.

The Underwood twitched—its carriage shunted forward. *Shunk.* A single key seemed to rise on its own.

Pause…

Clack.

Another followed.

Clack.

Clack.

Boniface stirred in his sleep, brow twitching, lips mumbling some inaudible prayer.

A final key dropped, without human touch. A single sheet waited, gripped in the machine's jaws.

Boniface woke. He rubbed his eyes, blinked. The Underwood was there, patient, watching, a fresh page curled in its carriage.

He walked barefoot across the freezing floor. Hesitated. Drew the paper free.

The words were stark. Dark. Perfect.

Bone-sky morning, her silence a wound / that blooms in the corner of the room…

His heart thudded. "I didn't write this."

He sat down, repeating, "a world unmoving, dust in the mouth / lips whispering secrets to the dark…"

Every morning for thirty-six days, Boniface woke to find a new poem in the typewriter's jaws. Each one sharper, darker, more beautiful than the last.

His ritual became sacred: rising, pulling the page, copying it into emails sent to editors, never explaining the source.

One lukewarm reply came: *Interesting. Send more.*

He sent everything.

Days turned into weeks.

Boniface checked his email. Nothing came.

Out of options and short of money, Boniface signed up to Midnight Editions—a bargain-bin digital press that promised reach, readership, and success for a yearly fee of £8.89. He pressed submit, watching his new poems vanish into the endless stream of new titles, the site assuring him he'd joined a community of writers on the rise.

He titled the collection *Echoes on Paper*. The cover was stark: a shadowed photograph of the Underwood.

At first, nothing happened. Then the reviews began.

These are Sylvia Plath's poems. Word for word.

A shameless fraud. Plagiarism.

Boniface's hands trembled as he scrolled through the accusations. His stomach churned. He opened Google and typed the first line of a poem.

There it was. Sylvia Plath. Line for line.

In a frenzy, he logged back in to Midnight Editions, hammering at the keyboard, desperate to delete the collection. The page froze, refreshed, froze again—too late. The words were already out there, copied, screenshotted, shared.

The fear hollowed him. His chest thumped with the terror that this machine had betrayed him, that it would not stop.

Rain poured down as Boniface stumbled out, cradling the Underwood against his chest.

Gideon & Finch was dark, its window lifeless. Behind the glass, a crooked *CLOSED* sign was barely visible through the condensation. He set the typewriter on the step.

He rose, turned, and vanished into the storm.

The next day, the typewriter appeared in Gideon & Finch's window, its enamel streaked by rain. A handwritten label was attached: *Underwood No. 5. Used by a Poet. No Provenance. £50.*

A young woman paused outside, rain dripping from her umbrella, pooling in circles at her feet.

She pushed the door open. The bell dinged, and the door closed behind her. She shook off her umbrella, droplets scattering across the scuffed floorboards, and stepped deeper into the gloom. The floorboards creaked as she approached the typewriter. It sat on its display, dark and silent. Her hand reached out to touch it…

"Beautiful, ain't she?"

The proprietor emerged from the dimness, a gaunt figure with shoulders that slumped, his cardigan a few sizes too big. With his fingernail, pale as bone, he rapped against the table.

"Works like a dream, it does. They say it belonged to someone famous. You know Plath, the poet? The one that stuck her head in the gas oven?"

The woman froze. "Plath?"

The proprietor shrugged, his grin never faltering. "No proof, no paper trail. Just talk. But a good story doesn't need the truth, does it?"

The Boy Who Ate Books

It began with a page—an innocent slip torn from *Treasure Island*. He wanted to taste the adventure, the salt air, the hidden treasure. He ripped a strip from page eleven and slipped it onto his tongue. The ink was bitter, the paper dry, dissolving to paste as he chewed.

He gagged. Panic clawed at his chest. He closed his eyes, desperate for air, and burped—just as, for a heartbeat, fear sparked in him at the shadow of a man with a tarred pigtail standing at a harbour's edge. The vision flickered and vanished, leaving Samuel shaken.

He tore a second strip from page eleven. It went down easier this time. A warmth spread through him—the promise of adventure taking root. He tore another strip, then another, and another. He mouthed, "*I remember him as if it were yesterday, as he came plodding to the inn door, his sea-chest following behind him in a hand-barrow…*"

The next morning at breakfast, he arrived with a torn book page clutched in one hand, his jaw moving slowly.

"What are you eating?" his mother asked.

"Nothing," he said. "Just a page from a book." He scratched his nose and asked her for a "*hearty swig o' grog*".

She stared at him as if he'd lost his wits. "Books are meant to be read, not eaten, Samuel!" she laughed.

It was Saturday—no school, a day set aside for reading. The taste of *Treasure Island* still clung to his tongue, and he was hungry for more.

Upstairs in the family reading room, he sat cross-legged on the overstuffed settee. A scatter of books lay at his side. From *The Wind in the Willows* he tore a page, chewed, swallowed. Then another from *Oliver Twist*, and one more from *Biggles Flies East*. Each carried its own flavour: the first green-sweet and loamy, the second bitter with soot and iron, the third sharp with spice and the faint burn of oil.

Though his hunger grew, he soon found the stories did not fill his stomach. Instead, they gathered in his mind, where voices pressed close and characters began to take shape.

Day by day, Samuel's words shifted. One morning he greeted his mother with a flourishing bow and a booming "*Good morrow!*" fresh from *Hamlet*. By lunchtime, after swallowing pages of *Heart of Darkness*, "*the horror!*" slipped out under his breath. From the kitchen doorway she watched, uneasy, as he gnawed at the corner of *War and Peace*, gagged, and spat out fragments of Napoleon's discourse with a faint, dismissive burp.

At school, his friends were the first to notice the growing changes. Samuel, once the quiet boy hunched at the back, gradually transformed into a one-man theatre. One day he was Heathcliff, brooding over his desk, muttering about cursed moors; the next he was Sir Lancelot, puff-chested and gallant, demanding imaginary duels in the playground.

Teachers thought he was acting out—until they heard him pour out whole passages from *Moby Dick* and *The Divine Comedy*, as if the stories were living through him.

But change never stays secret for long. By Tuesday, the rumours had begun.

"Samuel's acting weird," a girl giggled. "Keeps challenging people to duels. He's like… possessed."

His English teacher was intrigued. In the middle of a discussion on *Macbeth*, Samuel's eyes locked on an empty space above the blackboard, and he delivered, "*Is this a dagger which I see before me?*"

The teacher alerted the headmaster. The headmaster summoned his mother.

And there, in the cluttered office, wringing the strap of her handbag, she stuttered the only explanation she could. "He… he… he's eating b-b… books."

Samuel's habit reached the ears of Tom Harrington, a local journalist known for chasing oddities. He had once reported on a turnip shaped like the Queen's head and a man who claimed his dog spoke French. But a boy eating books—this was different.

During their video-recorded interview, Samuel chewed on the edge of a book as he spoke. "The words taste different depending on the book," he explained matter-of-factly. "Shakespeare is rich and heavy, like roast beef and gravy. Dickens is dry like toast left too long in the sun. Hemingway is sharp—his words cut like cold citrus."

Tom jotted down notes, sensing he had something memorable to report.

The Boy Who Eats Books was published a day later and went viral overnight.

By morning, the local newspaper's web page was drowning in traffic, dragged down by clickbait headlines slapped across the internet.

Boy Claims Shakespeare Tastes Like Roast Beef

Is Book-Eating the Next TikTok Trend?

The Literary Diet: Could YOU Survive on Nothing but Words?

Clips of Samuel's interview spread fast. One showed him chewing the corner of a book while describing Hemingway as "citrusy and cold". The buzz grew louder. Talk shows wanted him. Food critics weighed in. A celebrity chef offered to design a literary tasting menu. A furious librarian recorded a rant about "the sanctity of books". An indie publisher announced, "100% organic, artisanal poetry prints—safe for consumption!"

Samuel ignored it all. He fixed his breakfast: a bowl of shredded pages of Kipling's *If*, drowned in chocolate milk. "*If you can keep your head when all about you are losing theirs…*" he slurped. After breakfast, he flipped open *The Life of Pi*, running a finger over a page, wondering if it would taste of salt and survival.

Invited onto morning shows, he amazed audiences. The news about the book-eating boy spread far and wide, catapulting him into the national spotlight. Viewers from across the country sent in pages from their favourite books, challenging Samuel's extraordinary palate. With each correct answer, his fame grew—and so did his confidence in his peculiar gift.

He was invited to perform at the Cheltenham Literary Festival and responded with a provocative request: "I want to be in a gilded cage."

The organisers hesitated—was this performance art? *Was it ethical?* But the spectacle was too tempting to resist. And so, in the grand hall, a golden birdcage was set at centre stage, and inside it sat Samuel, blindfolded, with one ankle chained to the floor like a character from a gothic novel.

Throngs of literary enthusiasts gathered, throwing pages into the cage. His mother picked up the pages and handed them to Samuel. One spectator, eager to stump him, tossed in a worn sheet from *The Man Who Was Thursday* by G.K. Chesterton. Samuel sniffed, chewed, and announced not only the title and author but also the exact passage—a conversation between Syme and Gregory on the philosophy of anarchism.

Next, a page fluttered down from Virginia Woolf's *To the Lighthouse*—the moment Mrs Ramsay contemplates the fragile complexity of life and relationships. Samuel's eyes blinked with recognition as he digested the words, then recited them in a voice laced with melancholy that silenced the sceptics.

A man with ginger hair folded a page from *Finnegans Wake* into a paper jet and thrust it towards Samuel. It glided into the cage. Would he falter here? Samuel took his time, letting the tangled prose sit on his tongue. His brow furrowed. Then, the words flowed: "This is a stream of consciousness… a blending of dreams and waking thought… It is James Joyce unspooling the logic of the subconscious."

Someone in a pink 1970s catsuit stepped forward and threw in a crumpled page from *Maus* by Art Spiegelman. Samuel held it. He chewed and paused, before stating gravely, "This is a graphic novel. The weight of memory is in the ink. This passage is about a son trying to understand his father's pain."

In the quiet days following the festival, Samuel wandered through his house, restless. Fame had brought an endless supply of books—gifts from admirers and strangers who'd heard of his strange talent. Yet, he felt the words no longer held the same magic. The excitement of discovery had vanished. Now he wanted something more—a singular book that could complete him.

One afternoon, on a whim, Samuel remembered his father mentioning a book that had challenged him. Curious, he stepped into the reading room. On a shelf, he spotted the book: a leather-bound copy of *Pilgrim's Progress*. He pulled it down, feeling its weight in his hands.

Samuel opened it. Then, he tore off a corner from page thirty-seven and popped it into his mouth. The words differed from the others. For the first time, his habit of nibbling felt less like a game and more like a quest. It was as if he were searching for answers within the story and within himself. He paid closer attention to the pilgrim's journey, feeling the lessons and burdens as his own. The taste was dry as ashes, yet strangely alive. The story settled in him where words had never dared to reach.

Page after page, Samuel devoured the story, his eyes wild, his hunger desperate. With each bite, he felt himself dissolving, becoming the pilgrim: lost, wounded, and yearning for change. The journey pressed him deeper, reshaping him in ways he had feared to imagine, as if, at last, he was drawing near to understanding himself.

He looked up from the empty cover, his eyes watery, face drawn with exhaustion. "My burden is great," he whispered, voice barely audible. He slumped forward, every swallowed word settling over him, heavy as sorrow.

His mother found him there, peaceful on the overstuffed settee, the hollow book resting across his chest—only the front and back covers remained. In his hand, pinched between two fingers, was a scrap of paper. The ink was smudged.

Thus far did I come laden with my sin; nor could anything ease the grief that I was in, till I came hither.

The Sommelier of Soil

Dennis knelt in the allotment beneath a sky unsettled, out of joint with the season. His wrists shone with sweat; his palms pressed into soil still damp with yesterday's rains. Beside him, a glove lay collapsed, as if it had crawled there and died.

Without knowing why, he lifted a pinch of soil to his lips. It entered him like a secret: grit against enamel, the iron taste of buried centuries, a sweetness that did not belong to food. He did not ask himself why. Perhaps the earth wanted to be remembered in this way—by dissolving into the body of the one who tended it. He grabbed a sand clod and shoved it in his mouth. Earthier, deeper, like tasting a buried memory. Maybe oak leaves, maybe ancient compost. It was damn weird, but somehow right.

He moved slowly across the allotment. At the edge of his wildflower patch, the soil was drier. Another taste. Sharper this time, what he thought was green tomatoes and clover. Near the compost heap, the flavour changed again—something like a warm Cabernet Sauvignon.

He sat between mint and chives, knees up, arms resting, confusion and awe swirling through him. He wondered aloud, voice thick with emotion, "What the fuck—are there hidden stories or poems buried at my feet?"

The sky cleared. Birds in the hedgerows fell silent; time to head home for a beer. Slinging his canvas bag over his shoulder, Dennis paused at the allotment storage box. He grabbed four small glass jars full of seeds, emptied them onto the compost heap, placed the jars in his bag, then picked up his garden trowel. On the way home, he stopped at four spots to gather soil, refilling the jars.

Dennis began collecting small soil samples wherever he went, tasting, sniffing them like snuff, swirling them on his tongue like a sommelier.

He scribbled in his notebook after each tasting, trying to translate the taste into words. First, they were simple labels—sandy, coarse, bitter, dry. But as days passed, the soil demanded more precise language. Dennis's descriptions became ambitious: iron clinging to his throat, loam's crumble, ash of burned scrubland.

Around ten days after his soil tasting started, Dennis stood barefoot at the edge of his allotment, boots gripped tightly in his hands. He tossed the boots onto the compost heap—*goodbye, motherfuckers.* Turning away, he left the allotment's crops to rot. He dined solely on the earth's dark broth: leaf litter, humus, and the black crumble of lignin. Each handful became his sustenance and obsession. His commitment to the soil deepened.

This was his new beginning.

Seasons passed as Dennis's new life unfolded. He gathered, tasted, and wrote notes on each experience wherever his mind took him. He walked the paths, towpaths, canals, and farm roads barefoot, jars and trowel clinking in his bag. Each step was a pact with the earth, each journey a pilgrimage. Spring met him with hedgerows in bloom; summer baked the ground until it cracked beneath his heels. In autumn, he walked through leaves that crunched loudly; in winter, he pressed on over earth frozen to his skin.

People began to notice. They waited at gates or lingered in village lanes, curious about the man with clay on his soles and jars clinking like hidden bells. They watched him pause, stoop, and taste. Children copied him in play—scooping, sampling, tasting.

The market days drew near. On Saturday morning, Dennis arrived early. He set up his stall between the florist and the honey man, arranging his collection of glass jars—each filled with a different soil, each labelled in his careful hand. A small painted sign read: *Let me tell you the secrets of your soil.* Beside the jars, he set out his battered notebook, open to a page of scribbled soil poems.

People wandered by, some curious, others bemused. A few stopped, clutching little jars or tins, hoping for a taste of Dennis's odd wisdom.

Dennis was lost in a line of poetry, head bent, pen hovering above the page. He didn't look up until a soft clink sounded on the table—a battered old tea tin set down.

He glanced up. The woman standing before him had silver-grey hair tumbling loose, a small stud in her nose, bare feet dusted with earth. Her eyes held a playful challenge. "What does this tell you?"

Dennis unscrewed the tin, pinched some soil, and tasted. He let it settle, closed his eyes, then picked up his pen and quickly wrote a few lines in his notebook—words spilling out in small, slanting letters. When he finished, he tore the page free and handed it to her.

She read the poem aloud, voice soft but clear.

"this patch remembers
hands tangled (midnight)
warmth pressed deep
hips and roots entwined
breath buried in humus
the hush of skin
and nothing—
forgets."

The woman's eyes widened, a glimmer of surprise and understanding flickering deep, her smile turning bittersweet as she lowered the page. Her words trembled with emotion. "Soil never forgets, does it?" she said, as if the truth surprised her too.

Dennis smiled softly, feeling a quiet sense of connection. For a moment, neither spoke. The woman tucked the poem into her bag, her expression still touched by wonder, then she turned away and moved on to the honey stall.

Dennis wiped his hands and looked up. A slight girl stood between the honey-tasters and the florist. He caught her eye and nodded gently—it was her turn. She stepped forward, shoes left neatly beside her, bare feet shifting on the cobblestones. Her hair was loosely braided. She scuffed at the ground, eyes darting up at Dennis and then quickly down. At last she drew close enough to speak, her voice barely above a whisper. "Would you try mine?" Her cheeks flushed, as if she feared her request might be too much.

Dennis smiled, careful with the jar, pinched a bit of dirt, and set it on his tongue. Eyes closed, he tasted slowly, as if sifting secrets. Then he asked softly, "What's your name?"

"Claudia," she whispered.

"Long ago, your garden had a magic stream. On full moons, the fairies would come out—they'd whirl among the flowers and whisper, 'Grow, flowers, grow.' If you listen close, you might still hear them. Especially on quiet nights."

The girl gasped, hugging the jar close to her chest as if Dennis's words offered her comfort and protection. Her eyes shone.

A farmer approached Dennis. "You know you can't live on soil alone?"

Dennis met his gaze. "Can't you? The soil tells the secrets of your fields—if you listen."

The farmer shook his head and walked away.

As autumn slipped into winter and days shortened, ordinary concerns faded. Dennis lost himself in tasting hour after hour, cataloguing every grain. The soil's hold deepened. His shed became a chapel: shelves brimming with jars, each one holding a sliver of soil, a fragment of time. The jars were reliquaries, each one a patch of the earth captured, sealed, and translated into verse.

He lifted one, *New Forest 50°55'33.11" N, 1°39'40.75" W*, and read aloud:

"Deep hooves press stories
into the loam
wind threads through oak & pine
(whispers of riders long gone)
touch the earth & it holds firm
it does not rush
does not crumble
waits, ancient & sure."

He moved along the row, fingers brushing a jar filled with soil collected from where the land met the sea. *Compton Bay 50°39'22.24" N, 1°28'07.49" W.*

"red cliffs weep into the sea
bones of giants, pressed into time
footprints fade beneath salt & sky
the tide chews at history
& swallows it whole
but here, between rock & foam,
the past is still red on your hands."

Further along the shelf sat a darker sample, one he had gathered at dusk. *Winchester 51°03'46.06" N, 1°18'33.39" W.*

"this dirt is patient
it waits beneath footsteps & prayers
tastes of limestone & quiet grief

of old bones shifting deeper
of candle wax melted into stone
hold it on your tongue
and you will hear the choir still singing."

He traced his fingertips along the ridges of another jar: *Portsmouth 50°48'06.47" N, 1°06'36.32" W.*

"this is not soil, it is
iron ground to dust
salt caught in brickwork
hands blackened with industry
taste the air—
gunpowder, rust, old ghosts
but never let it rest."

And then, one of his most treasured samples, *Tennyson Down 50°39'59.28" N, 1°32'29.40" W.* He opened the jar before reading out:

"the wind does not stop here
it pulls at the cliffs,
at your breath, at your words
the white path crumbles, step by step
bones of poets
sown deep in the chalk
their voices sink into the tide."

By midsummer, the soil was bitter on Dennis's tongue. Where once he tasted oak, compost, riverbank, now it coated his mouth with metal and ash. Birds no longer called from the hedgerows. Bees stumbled over petals and dropped.

Fields stood sullen, seed refusing to take. Nights flared with strange light on the horizon; mornings pressed down with silence.

He kept tasting. His notebook filled with jagged lines: *iron dust, hollow loam, shallow-buried smoke.* The jars in his satchel clinked like muffled bells as he walked barefoot through the lanes.

The change came without storm. Leaves browned before their time. Orchards flowered and shed, fruit never swelling. Rivers shrank to channels of silt. Villages emptied as if everyone had stepped out at once. Dennis stayed crouched among his jars, tongue black with soil, bent over his pages.

Then no birds. No bees. No voices on the road. Only the dry rasp of wind across the fields.

Years slid past in silence. The jars gathered dust, the notebooks curled at their edges. The shed sagged into itself.

At last the rain returned—first scattered drops that vanished on impact, then enough to soften the cracks. Shoots pressed up through the shed floor, curling between jars, roots threading through the pages. Wildflowers rose where his knees had pressed the earth, colour spreading across the ruin: yellow, violet, white.

A Stranger in Kensington

In the weeks after the stranger arrived, a sleek van emblazoned with the Christie's logo became a fixture at Queen's Gate Terrace. Neighbours, accustomed to the area's discreet opulence, watched intently. Deliveries appeared with clockwork precision: objects shrouded in canvas with the silhouettes of antique frames or sculptural oddities, crates bearing customs seals and fragile labels hinted at provenance and staggering worth. With each arrival, the enigma of the basement flat's new occupant deepened.

What could one man be doing with such treasures hidden beneath the street?

No invitations were issued, and no explanations came from the stranger. His movements were watched, dissected, and spun into gossip blooming through the terrace, casting him as anything from a collector of oddities to something far more menacing.

One Wednesday before dawn, when the streets of South Kensington lay leeched of colour and the lamps paled as night receded, he slipped from the flat without a sound. He walked south, passing shuttered cafés and bolted garden gates. The river's scent closed in around him. At Albert Bridge he slowed, and beneath its span he halted. In the half-light, he watched a skiff approach—a lone rower silhouetted against the wan Thames.

Without a sound, he reached forward and took the worn Gladstone bag from the boatman's hands. He turned and walked home in silence through the mist-veiled streets.

He locked the door when he got in. He placed the bag on the antique worktop, opened it, and retrieved a velvet pouch containing a Schott & Genossen jar filled with a thick, murky liquid. He whispered, "Rana esculenta," and set it down.

At the centre of the room stood a monastery table, carved from oak and polished to a soft, timeworn sheen. Thirteen Imperial Gilden porcelain bowls sat on the table, their smooth surfaces reflecting the light. Six bowls graced each of the long sides, and the thirteenth commanded attention at the head. Green-enamel Benjamin pendant lamps cast a soft glow over each place setting. Two cables per lamp—an anode and a cathode—were suspended above each bowl and their ends descended through twin apertures in the glass cloches that covered the porcelain.

He picked up the Schott & Genossen jar. Taking a pipette, he drew the viscous liquid out and dispensed a precise, equal measure into each of the first twelve bowls until the jar was empty, careful not to spill a drop.

He lowered each of the anodes and cathodes into the liquid. Then, he flipped a switch. The room filled with a low, vibrating hum.

By May, the experiment shifted from clinical procedure to something out of a grim fairy tale. Swollen tadpoles churned in the broth.

By June, slick, mottled bodies writhed in the bowls, budding limbs flexed.

Nightly, the stranger's chant grew louder. "Rana esculenta. Rana esculenta. Ra-naaaaaaaa es-culentaaaaaaaaaaaah."

Culling of the frogs took place daily—the weak, the runts, disposed of in ways no one cared to name.

The survivors had become something beyond frogs. Their hind legs were elongated and muscular, proportions balanced, symmetry exact. Their bodies showed a ripeness that invited use. Their eyes gleamed with sharp, unsettling intelligence. By Midsummer's Eve, there were twelve perfect specimens.

From the drawer he drew it: *Le Guide Culinaire*, Escoffier's gospel. Its leather hide was swollen with age, letters pressed in gold as though branded by some divine hand. He laid it upon a wooden lectern like a priest setting out a breviary. Gloved fingers parted the pages until they found their sacrament—*Cuisses de Nymphe à l'Aurore,* 'Thighs of the Nymph at Dawn'.

At the Boos butcher's block, he took up his couteau à désosser. The frogs lay waiting, bellies up like sacrifices.

One by one he traced the seam of the hip. Steel kissed joint; tendon loosened with a flick and a twist. Bone surrendered. Flesh parted. Pale legs, translucent and veined faintly in rose, glimmered on the board as though still pulsing with memory. He laid each back gently into the bowl. The liquid embraced the wound, and the legs began, impossibly, to knit and swell again.

He poured Jersey cow's milk into a shallow dish—cool, thick, maternal—and lowered the severed limbs into its velvet depths. While they softened, he prepared the court bouillon. Salon 1905 Blanc de Blancs cracked open in a gasp, poured into copper like liquid stars. Tarragon bruised beneath his fingers. Bay leaves snapped like brittle bones. Amalfi zest ignited the air with a sharp kiss of lemon.

From a small glass jar came Fleur de Sel de Guérande. Crystalline as diamonds, it fell grain by grain like the glitter of constellations. White Sarawak pepper followed, ground between his palms, a spice-flower releasing its fire. Appellation d'Origine Protégée Échiré butter bubbled in the pan, golden as dawn. The milk-bathed legs were lifted out and dabbed dry on Irish linen, their flesh trembling, quivering like a lover beneath his fingertips. He dusted them in Hokkaido flour, shook them clean, and lowered the first into the molten butter. The flesh tightened, gasped, crisping into a perfect gilded crust. One by one they followed, sizzling, turning amber. The scent rose in a narcotic curl: caramelised butter, browning flesh, herbs sighing in the steam.

He flipped them, undersides bronzed, bodies transformed, then arranged them on a warm porcelain platter as relics awaiting consecration.

In the same pan, Bordier butter released its truffle ghost—earthy and delirious. Roscoff shallots and Lautrec garlic wept sweetness into the air. They softened to translucence, golden at the edges. Then, uncorked with a reverent twist, came the 1996 Château d'Yquem. Honeyed amber spilled into the pan like sunlight wrung from the sky. It hissed and spat, reduced to syrup, thickening into a splendour beyond reason. Imperial Heritage Ossetra caviar broth deepened it, the sea whispering through the sweetness.

In a separate bowl, he beat Bresse yolks into Normandy cream—liquid sun, trembling gold. He trickled them into the pan. The mixture transformed into silk. A blush of Vesuvius tomato, a tear of Amalfi lemon, a final pinch of smoked paprika, then the sauce bloomed into the precise shade of dawn.

The legs were returned, cloaked now in their velvet vestments, drinking in the sauce. He laid them on a bed of Cristal champagne jelly, translucent and trembling. Then the last flourish: Périgord truffle, shaved thin, fell like black snow over gilded flesh, dark prophecy scattered upon a rising sun.

The dish was complete. Done. Perfect.

The stranger reached up, fingers brushing the cool brass of the pendant above the large bowl at the head of the table. He found the switch. After a soft click, the green enamel shade bloomed with light. He carried the platter forward, the sauce glistening under the lamps, and tilted it gently, sliding the gilded flesh into the waiting bowl.

He poured 1921 Château Haut-Brion Blanc from a crystal decanter. The delicate Baccarat glass felt cool against his fingertips as he raised it to his lips. The wine was a revelation. Notes of honeyed apricot, toasted almond, and a whisper of sea salt followed. He sipped, closing his eyes as the flavours unfolded—a prelude to the feast before him.

He lifted the first leg delicately between finger and thumb, brought it to his lips, and bit. The first taste was pure transcendence—velvet sauce, flesh yielding in tenderness, flavours unfolding like a symphony on his tongue.

The frogs watched from their bowls as he prepared for his second leg.

Raising his hands, he intoned a Latin prayer: "Gratias ago tibi, Domine, pro dono vitae renatae. Benedictio mea in Rana esculenta." He traced a holy sign across his chest and chanted again softly before taking a bite. The flesh dissolved on his tongue, the chaudfroid rich and delicate.

On the next bite, his throat clenched. A shard of bone caught him, sharp and unforgiving. He gasped and clawed at his throat, the fork clattering to the table. "Sancte Deus, miserere mei!" he rasped, stumbling back as the room tilted. He collapsed to the stone floor.

The frogs stirred.

Their new limbs flexed, muscles swelling as the electric current urged them on. One creature leapt and struck the glass dome; it toppled with a crash, wires snapping free. Another creature followed, then another, until the cloches clattered across the table. Glass shattered and scattered in every direction.

Freed, they dragged themselves over porcelain and copper. Claws scratched wood as they leapt from the table to the floor.

Their jaws parted, revealing rows of fine, needle-sharp teeth, birthed by alchemy.

They turned as one, closing on the stranger at the room's centre.

And then, they feasted.

Nolite Inquinare Plumas Eorum

"Why am I called Corvida, Grandpa?"

She watched as he rested his shears against the hedge. He said, "Your mother said it means raven-like—a name destined for strange and shadowy paths."

Her grandfather had raised her from infancy. Her father, a soldier, was killed weeks before her birth. Her mother withered soon after, slipping into silence and gone before Corvida's first birthday. Whatever grief her grandfather carried, he kept sealed, drowning most evenings in whiskey and the quiet glow of the hearth.

Corvida's childhood unfolded in a weathered Victorian cottage between Guildford and Woking. Her grandfather, the Wetherby estate's quiet steward, drifted each day through emerald lawns and gnarled, story-laden trees. She trailed in his wake, learning the language of roots and earth, the manor's silhouette always haunting the horizon of her world.

At twelve, she was sent to the manor with a message. She stepped into the hallway. A kestrel hung in the air, poised in mid-dive, every feather outlined by dim light. A fox stood snarling, its glassy eyes in perpetual challenge, while pheasants exuded lacquered elegance. The air seemed to hum with a stillness that watched her. She reached for the pheasants' plumage.

A voice shattered the tableau: "Don't dirty their feathers!"

She spun, startled.

Charles Wetherby leaned in the doorway—golden-haired, poised on manhood's edge. "You want to see more? I'll show you."

Over the next season, Charles took an unsettling interest in Corvida. He offered her sugared almonds, let her shadow him on hunts, and praised her cleverness in ways no one else ever had. Sometimes, he invited her back into the manor, leading her through the grand halls under the guise of sharing his world of curiosities. But his charm twisted into cruelty in the hidden corridors and dim alcoves far from watchful eyes. He stole pieces of her she didn't yet understand.

Corvida told no one. Who would believe the groundskeeper's strange, silent granddaughter over a Wetherby? She locked the truth inside herself, and in that sealed place something else began to grow—a quiet fixation on the stillness of the manor's trophies.

They never flinched, never bled, never spoke. She began to think of them as armour—a way to pin the instant of harm in place, to hold it long enough that it could no longer press close. In the long, unspoken hours, the idea hardened.

Soon she began collecting roadkill and woodland remains, cradling each lost creature and murmuring apologies only they could hear. Her first efforts were awkward: a magpie with crooked wings, feathers stiffened by glue; a hare whose fur sloughed off in rancid clumps. The shed became a chamber of decay, its stench weaving into her hair and clothes, the air heavy with rot and plaster dust. Yet she pressed on, unwavering, every failure a lesson sewn into her fingers.

Two years later, at fourteen, Corvida discovered it—*Practical Taxidermy* by Montagu Browne, wedged on a low shelf in the village's second-hand shop, its cover worn thin. The book was late-Victorian, its pages close-set with diagrams and precise instructions. She read standing in the narrow aisle, lips moving over strange words: *arsenical soap, plaster of Paris, wire through the wing-bone.* In the margins, someone had scrawled notes in a darker hand—recipes, corrections, fragments that hinted at older knowledge.

The price was impossible: more than a month of her grandfather's wages. She lingered, eyes flicking to the shopkeeper each time he shifted. When he disappeared into the back room, she slipped it under her jacket, pressing it flat against her chest, and walked out into the grey street, heart hammering louder than her steps.

After dinner, she went to her room and drew the lamp close. She opened the book, its dense text and diagrams stark in the yellow glow. She copied passages into a notebook, sketching where the instructions demanded it, and mouthing words until her eyes closed. Night after night the same pattern returned: read, copy, remember.

Her tools were plain: wire, tow, stout twine, a few sharp knives. She worked with what her grandfather had left lying around over the years, following Browne's instructions step by step—a cut along the breastbone, skin eased carefully back, plaster pressed into hollow places. The book never left her bench. She copied its notes in her own hand, sketched diagrams in the margins, repeating the odd phrases until they lived in her mouth. Sometimes her grandfather stood in the doorway, arms folded, saying little, watching her bent to her work beneath the lamp.

The shed transformed into her sanctuary, a reliquary crowded with drying bones and skins pinned like strange prayers. Nothing yielded easily. Skins split, stitches unravelled, a single slip of the blade could undo hours of work. She kept her failures in a box beneath the bench—wings without bodies, tails severed from heads—silent tokens of patience's price.

And then, once in a while, a creature was completed: a magpie whose glass eyes caught the lamplight, a hare held forever in the moment before its leap. They were hers now, uncanny and whole.

By the time she turned seventeen, Corvida was apprenticed to a taxidermist in Godalming. The workshop sat behind a narrow shopfront, its windows crowded with creatures held in their poses: an owl in flight, wings stretched wide; a fox frozen mid-snarl, teeth bared at some invisible threat.

Under her mentor's gaze, she learned to articulate skeletons, set glass eyes to catch the light, and smooth feathers into order. But something else showed in Corvida's work. A rabbit crouched as if caught in a tightening snare. A trout twisted on its mount, gills flared, gasping at absent water. A pheasant's wings spread wide, plumage bright, terror sealed in its stance. Her mentor praised her skill but kept a distance, unsettled by the edge in her creations.

In the summer of 1983, the Eurythmics' "Sweet Dreams (Are Made of This)" rode the airwaves. And at number 17, Cambridge Crescent in Camden, a nineteen-year-old Corvida stopped. She dropped her suitcase at her feet and adjusted her backpack. The house she faced was a tall building with a stucco façade, a green door with a fanlight above it, tidy iron railings bordering the sidewalk, and a brass plaque reflecting the sunlight. This would be her home now, with her last remaining aunt, her grandfather having given the move his blessing. The flat still carried the ghost of her aunt's late husband, a property man who had made his wealth in Camden's rows of houses.

The streets of Camden peeled away the quiet girl she once was and clothed her in something fierce. Within months, her arms blossomed with Victorian tattoos—stags, foxes, owls, snakes—each etched with the meticulous care she gave her craft. A nose ring caught the light, her hair turned the blue-black of a raven's wing, and corsets sculpted her into a silhouette that was equal parts Victorian relic and punk rebellion.

To Corvida, Camden itself was a living taxidermy: misfits remade, old skins shed, new ones worn until they bled. In its shadowy pubs and backroom stages, she discovered her tribe.

In the second or third winter after unpacking her bags at her aunt's flat, Corvida returned to the village in the valley to stand at her grandfather's graveside. The church bells tolled. Away from the sadness of the service, miners marched through towns with banners blackened in coal dust.

In the week her aunt was lowered into the earth, now several years after her arrival in Camden, the newsstands screamed of towers falling. The service took place in the churchyard of St Michael's, Camden Town—a narrow Gothic revival chapel, its stone shadowed beneath the plane-tree canopy. Corvida sat alone; two figures at the back murmured their condolences, strangers whose grief she did not share.

She told her employers at The Noble Hare that she was leaving to set up on her own. They argued, coaxed, tried to talk her down, but the decision was set. The farewell ended up at the Hawley Arms, vodka and Red Bulls knocked back until the walls tilted. By morning her head throbbed with it all—the drink, the noise, the sense that she had finally stepped out on her own.

Back at Cambridge Crescent, transformation took root. The basement was gutted and reborn: new benches, shelves multiplying, lights strung to chase away the lingering gloom, drawers for bone and beak, cabinets of glass eyes waiting in patient silence.

Upstairs, the wide sitting room was stripped to bare boards and then dressed anew: plinths and cases rose, linen curtains softened the light. The house split itself without protest—workshop below, gallery above—until it belonged not to her aunt's memory, but to Corvida alone.

She sat at the table, a glass of orange juice half-finished beside *The Guardian*, its pages spread open. The headline above the fold read, *No officers to face charges over Menezes.* Beneath it, another story screamed of Lebanon—*Israel gears up for ground war.* She turned to the *Review* insert. There she was on the front page: a photograph of herself seated in her gallery, surrounded by her creations. The headline ran: *The Alchemy of Preservation.* She began to read.

Corvida Blackthorn transforms what is lost into what endures. In her hands, bone and hide become tableaux of motion and memory, animals set not in death but in continuation. Patrons travel across the country to commission her work, each creature rendered with uncanny fidelity to the spirit their owners remember…

A knock rattled the gallery door. She opened it, and Charles Wetherby stood there—temples dusted with grey, a paunch pressing against his tweed, the old entitlement still alive in the set of his jaw. He stared at the ink winding her arms, the corset's tight lines, the raven hair falling against her pale skin.

"Do I know you?" He tilted his head, eyes narrowing.

Corvida let the silence stretch, watching doubt flicker in his eyes. "Maybe. Camden's small. Faces cross."

"Strange," he muttered, brushing it aside. "I was told this is where to find unusual work."

"Then you're in the right place."

He dropped a canvas bag onto a display table, the glass domes rattling. With a smirk, he pulled free a saker falcon, its wings limp, head swinging by the neck.

"Uzbekistan. Took it myself. Rare bird." He chuckled, short and smug. "Better in your hands than left to rot."

"Let's see what I can do. But first—tea?"

He nodded once, eyes scanning the gallery.

"Sit."

She measured out the leaves, added sugar, and a trace of something ground so fine it vanished into the mix. She set the cup on the table; he raised it and inhaled, putting it to his lips.

He sipped. "Fresh. Sweet. Something more—almond?"

"Come. I'll show you the workshop."

She turned to the basement door. And Charles Wetherby followed.

Some time later, in the second week of August, Corvida placed a small handwritten sign in the living room window. *Closed for the summer.* She locked the front door and walked toward Mornington Crescent underground station.

Time moved on. Summer passed, and then autumn.

In the following weeks, his name flickered in the papers—missing, presumed abroad, rumours of scandal. Then the story ebbed.

Residents of Cambridge Crescent contacted the council.

The authorities forced the door of the abandoned house and descended into the basement. In the half-light stood a cage—iron twisted into the semblance of an aviary.

Years later, one of the council officials would post about it on social media.

'Fuck me… nothing prepares you. After we forced the door—me, two lads from housing, one from health & safety—we went down into that basement not knowing what we would find. there's a bloody cage, right in the middle, iron all twisted up into this aviary shape…

inside was a man. Or what used to be one. Totally naked and that pale blue colour of bodies like you see in those films with police forensic teams. His arms stretched like Jesus on the cross , - the shoulders looked torn loose, stitches running down them, like split open. His hands were like they had no flesh - just the bones. U could see the veins pressed under his legs, and his skin was covered in varnish with bubbles underneath. His mouth was open wide and his tongue hung out - one eye socket was empty, and the other stuffed with a light bulb. And his cock was gone like chopped off…

On his shoulder was a falcon. I thought it was real ,, Wings spread, every feather shining, talons buried clean into his collar. Its beak was red-gold, polished, perfect. The man's eye was in its one claw…. and threads still hanging from it. Looked like it had just been plucked.

And there was a fox between his legs - it also looked alive - like really alive. … the mans cock was hanging from its jaws black and shrivelled. The thing that fucked with my brain most was that across his chest there was this burnt in or carved in tattoo. Nolite inquinare plumas eorum. I googled it. it means Don't dirty their feathers…….

Oh, here's the sick part: the cage when we came in, it was beautiful. Proper craftsmanship - like it was meant for a cathedral."

Corvida sat on the sun-drenched terrace at La Corneille, a glass of red wine cradled in her earth-stained hands. Below, the Écrins Valley spilled out in silence and colour, green melting into blue, shadow dissolving into light. Behind her, the herb garden—sage, rue, belladonna—breathed and whispered in the wind.

Overhead a rook circled once, then landed on the iron chair opposite her.

It folded its wings.

Corvida did not stir.

The bird did not leave.

Poached

The man in the faded boiler suit sat perched on a green plastic bin outside the rhino enclosure at Regent's Park, a toy rhinoceros taped to his forehead with two strips of duct tape. Behind him buses hissed on wet roads, sirens rose and fell, but in front—through bars and glass—a black rhinoceros shifted in the mud, its breath rising pale in the cold. The man held a placard:

HELP ME BECOME A RHINO.

ALL DONATIONS WELCOME.

Families with pushchairs steered wide, pretending not to see. Two security men in high-vis jackets asked him to move on.

*

The only light in his flat came from the laptop screen, a faint glow caught on the rims of his thick glasses. His fingers tapped steadily, the keys sticky from use, each search peeling him deeper into a tunnel of obsession: *rhino anatomy, horn grafting, skull thickness human vs animal.*

Around him, posters of rhinos curled from damp walls, books on rhinos piled like Jenga towers, photocopied pages littered the floor. The edges of the light caught the flank of a ceramic rhino, the bent spines of conservation manuals, and dust thick as fur.

He sipped his concoction—tap water mixed with powdered roots, dried leaves from the Asian grocer, and something green he thought rhinos might chew. It stank of a compost heap and beetroot, and each sip made him gag, but he forced it down, muttering that it brought him closer to rhinos.

The laptop screen pulsed, lines of text swimming darker, a message buried deep in the back alleys of the dark web. He peered over the top of his glasses and read it once, then again.

REAL RHINO HORN AVAILABLE.

SERIOUS BUYERS ONLY.

He read the details. Then came a single tap—*SEND*—and it was done. The money gone, the message dispatched into a void of faceless traders. He sat back, listening to the tick of the kitchen clock.

Days dragged. He measured them in concoction glasses drained, in the thud of the letterbox that brought only bills, in the muffled parcels dumped for neighbours he'd never met.

There were two loud clacks at the letterbox, and when he stepped into the hall, he found a white card on the mat, handwritten in block capitals, the ink smudged with damp: *IT'S WAITING. KING'S CROSS—LOCKER 12. 493-781-206.*

He left right away.

At King's Cross he followed the signs to the parcel lockers by the newsagent; the keypad was greasy with a hundred fingers. He tapped in the nine digits and a green light blinked as a shallow door unlatched, revealing a shoebox wrapped in brown paper and cinched with grey tape. He slid it into his bag and walked back into the rain without looking round.

Back home, he set the box on the counter and slit the wrapping with a butter knife.

The horn lay in his hands at last.

It was scarred and ridged, the surface chipped where it had been hacked free. Life wrenched from a carcass and smuggled across oceans. He turned it slowly, tracing each scar, and then pressed it to his forehead.

The horn smelled of earth and blood. He carried it into the bathroom, flicked on the strip light. The mirror reflected a gaunt man with thick glasses and a blackened trophy pressed to his brow.

"This is the beginning."

The counter was soon cluttered with the contents of a second-hand surgeon's kit he'd bought off eBay—scalpels, clamps, curved needles, a bottle of disinfectant, rolls of gauze, rubber gloves, and a roll of duct tape—and from the dark web: blister packs of tramadol and codeine, vials of veterinary ketamine, syringes pre-loaded with lidocaine, a pouch of powdered sedative marked only with Cyrillic, antibiotics of uncertain origin, and a bundle of hollow needles sealed in crinkled plastic. He kept the zoo postcard from 1989—mother and calf—pinned above the sink.

He stood in front of the mirror, horn in one hand, scalpel in the other. His face stared back—pale, the skin stretched tight across his brow. He pressed the horn to his forehead, held it there for a second before placing it carefully on the rim of the bath.

On the laptop propped beside the sink, a YouTube video looped: a faceless pair of hands demonstrating how to inject local anaesthetic. *Pinch the skin, insert at forty-five degrees, draw back slightly, depress the plunger.* He mimicked each step, syringe trembling, eyes fixed on his own reflection in the mirror for reassurance.

The cold sting spread, then a numbness that was almost comfort. A bead of blood welled where the needle left its mark. He dropped the syringe into the sink

He raised the scalpel.

He hissed through his teeth as the cut tore, a hot line of red crawling down his face. It stung his eyes, the mirror blurred. He wiped at the flow with the back of his hand and cut again, deeper this time, flesh parting. The sink below splattered red.

The process was clumsy. Thread shook in his hands, needle stabbing through skin, tugging it tight around the horn's base. Knots bunched ugly against his flesh. He bound it all with duct tape, winding again and again, the tape squealing as it pulled free, sealing horn to head in a crude crown.

The mirror refused him. Breath misted the glass, streaked with threads of red, and in the blur a shifting mask gathered itself. His lips moved, forming words he could not hear, yet the face inside did not answer. From the centre a horn began to rise, pale and spectral, and the eyes that fixed on him were not his own—brighter, deeper, ancient, watching him from somewhere he could not reach.

Later he lay drenched in sweat, sheets sticking to his back, shivering, mumbling fragments of half-dreams. The wound pulsed, stitches leaking, flesh hot and furious. Pus crusted thick on the tape. He crammed antibiotics and painkillers into his mouth, swallowing them dry or with gulps of his foul green brew. Nights dissolved into heat and murmur. Hours stretched, folded, vanished. Sometimes he woke choking on soil, sometimes he felt the horn pressing from inside his skull, trying to break through.

On the eighteenth morning, his fingers found it. The horn no longer shifted. No longer separate. It was fixed, solid. It was his.

He leaned closer to the mirror, sweat dried to salt on his skin, stitches dark and stiff.

He stayed hidden for the winter, curtains drawn, the mirror his only witness. But the horn ached to be seen.

*

London felt strange, colder than he remembered, a cage of steel and glass. His shadow lurched across the stonework, stretching and warping.

He heard them before he saw them.

Laughter in the dark, thin and sharp. Figures slid into the light—three, maybe four—shadows, restless, hungry for something. They circled him, eyes drawn to the thing he had become.

The rhino sniffed the air. The rifle cracked. Thunder through bone. It staggered…

He tried to pull back, but they closed fast, hands slamming him into the wall.

Moonlight trembling on steel. The beast shuddered, ears flat, muscles trembling…

Steel flashed. Pangas—curved, brutal, blades catching the lamplight.

Another shot. Shoulder blown raw. The rhino sagged to its knees, breath tearing from its chest, a low grunt…

The first strike smashed bone.

The ground lurched beneath its weight. Chainsaw bit horn, shrieking louder than the rifle. The rhino bellowed, low and broken…

He screamed, knees buckling as steel tore into flesh and cartilage. They hacked at the horn with vicious rhythm, grunting, laughing.

Blood poured down its face, hot and heavy, soaking the dirt, turning dust to mud. Its tongue thick with iron, choking every breath.

Blood poured hot down his face, filled his mouth, spattered the wall. He went down hard, vision spinning, his body useless on the ground.

The horn wrenched free with a crack. One lifted it high, laughter sharp.

One of them wrenched the horn free with a sharp twist, holding it up like a trophy. “Easy money.”

They vanished into the bush.

They melted back into the shadows of the estate, their blades wet.

In the glass of its darkening eye, it saw a figure—half man, horned, bleeding, moving at the edge of the darkness. The shapes folded together…

He lay sprawled on the stonework, breath rattling, the taste of iron flooding his mouth, his blood soaking into the cracks. The pain thinned, shadows receding. In his dimming eye, he saw something vast and grey, steady as stone, silent as the earth.

He thought he had seen the beast…

The Last Plot

In the Parisian suburb of Saint-Jérôme, the allotments were sanctuaries, a place to dig your hands into the earth, older than memory, and summon life. Each allotment was a canvas, and the gardeners were its masters.

The allocation of allotments was cursed. The lottery system, though fair, was cruel: a name drawn from a weathered black box assigned you to wait—sometimes for a lifetime—before the allotment became yours. Even if you won, the soil remained forbidden until the current owner retired, moved away, or died.

The jewel of these sacred pieces of earth was parcelle 14 bis. Its immaculate rectangle of soil was bordered by rare blooms and herbs. Madame Léonie Durant, seventy-nine, had tended it for over half a century. Each bloom and herb reflected her dedication and pride in transforming the barren soil into beauty. Neighbours often spoke of the secretive zeal in her eyes, suggesting a private universe within her cherished garden.

The news that the allotment winners were to be announced filled Saint-Jérôme's market. A man in a black coat stepped onto the small wooden platform, rang a brass bell, and opened the black box. He drew out a folded sheet, smoothed it, and said, "Mesdames et Messieurs, the winner of this year's allotment lottery, who shall inherit parcelle 14 bis when it becomes available is… Les Trois Pelles."

The square was puzzled; then the name rolled around the stalls—*les trois pelles*—and laughter rose, some good-natured and some a little cruel. Someone shouted, "Bravo, Trois Pelles!"

The three men who had entered together glanced about as if the winners must be standing elsewhere. The bellman cleared his throat. "Registered as a cooperative of three," he added, consulting the page again, "submission time noted as 00h47 at Le Chat Gris," which prompted another ripple of amusement. "Signed by Vincent Dupont, Armand Lefèvre, and Pierre Callot."

They made a peculiar trio, mismatched in every way.

Thin and angular, Vincent Dupont had the nervous energy of a man who spent his days poring over tax returns. Driven by a longing for order and personal accomplishment, his dream was to create a garden as precise as his spreadsheets.

Armand Lefèvre, broad-shouldered and gruff, had once been a rugby player, the pride of Saint-Jérôme, until an injury left him with a limp. Still yearning for purpose and competition, he saw the allotment as his next field of conquest. Gardening, for him, was a way to claim new purpose and pride.

Pierre Callot, the undertaker, was the quietest of the three. He had a knack for coaxing life from things long thought dead; tending the allotment appealed to his sense of transforming what was lost.

Vincent clutched the paper. "It's ours, Pierre."

"Not yet. It's still hers."

That evening, the three sat in the dim light in Le Chat Gris, their drinks half-finished. A weary chanson drifted from the radio. The barman rinsed tumblers in a zinc sink; somewhere a spoon clinked against porcelain.

"She'll never leave," Vincent said.

"What if she had an accident?" Armand said. "She's old. People fall all the time."

Pierre's eyes strayed to the door, then back. "And if she doesn't?"

"Then… she falls anyway."

"We are not pushing an old woman into her petunias," Vincent said. "Try again."

"What if we make the allotment unpleasant?" Armand asked.

"How?"

"Pests. Rats in the compost, beetles in the soil."

"Where do you plan to find an army of beetles?"

"I know someone," Pierre said.

"No beetles," Vincent said. "Something subtler. Psychological."

"Like what?"

Armand kept his voice low as the barman walked past. "Plant something suspicious. Belladonna threading the tomatoes. Poison where she expects basil."

"A medieval *herboristerie* then," Vincent said.

Pierre picked up a toothpick. "Risky. What if she likes poisonous plants?"

"Does she look like the sort who does?"

"You never know."

"Fine. Next."

"Paranoia," Armand said. "Notes. Marks on the shed. Messages in the beds."

"What kind of messages?"

He dragged a finger through spilled wine and wrote: *PARTEZ.*

"Subtle," Pierre said.

"Yes," Vincent said, "she'll see that and abandon fifty years of work."

"Then we make it cursed."

Pierre almost smiled. "*Oh, j'aime bien ça.* Start small. A few dead birds, placed just so."

"Do you have dead birds, Pierre?"

"*Je connais quelqu'un.*"

"Then escalate," Armand said. "A ritual book, a ring of stones, maybe a goat skull—"

"Where would you get a goat skull?"

Pierre opened his mouth. Vincent cut in. "*Ne dis pas que tu connais quelqu'un.*"

"Or we tempt her away," Armand tried. "Tell her there's a better plot."

"Where?"

"Normandie."

"She's not a *vache*," Pierre said.

"Bretagne, then."

"She's seventy-nine," Vincent said. "She's not starting over."

"Buy her out?"

"With what money?"

Vincent stacked their empties at the edge of the table; the barman swapped them for fresh ones without being asked.

"All right," Pierre said. "Be practical. She's old. Maybe she just gets tired."

"Go on."

"She decides it's too much. We make it harder. Quietly."

Armand tore a beer mat into strips. "Shift her tools. Let her think she's forgetting."

"We 'help' badly," Pierre said. "Create problems she never had."

"It isn't murder," Vincent said. "It's… wearing her down."

"*Exactement.*"

Pierre raised his glass. "To ethical sabotage."

The rims touched.

"And if none of it works?" Vincent asked.

"Then we wait," Armand said.

"I hate this plan."

"Then we drink until a better one appears," Pierre said.

The chanson ended; the radio hissed and found another.

*

On an overcast evening, they struck. Madame Durant was kneeling among the *Orobanche alba*, lantern lighting the blooms.

"Bonsoir."

Madame Durant looked up, her bronze shears gleaming. "What do you want?"

"To admire the allotment," Armand said, stepping closer.

She looked them over: boots too clean for men who claimed a garden, hands without soil. "You're the ones from the market—Les Trois Pelles," she said, the name dry as dust. "If you're here to learn, keep to the path and mind the Saint-Jérôme bed; no one disturbs it on a waxing moon." She turned back to the *Orobanche alba*. "There's a spade by the shed—pass it here."

The spade struck the back of her head with a dull thud, and she crumpled into the soil she had tended for over fifty years.

They buried her beneath the Saint-Jérôme fern, patting the earth flat with their hands.

In the weeks that followed, Madame Durant's absence passed without comment. The villagers were accustomed to elders vanishing for a season—off to chase the sun, visit a far-flung niece, or slip quietly into the gentle riddles of old age.

But as the weeks stretched into months, the speculation began.

At the boulangerie, over the first croissants of the morning, Madame Gauthier said, "Perhaps she ran off to Italy. She always had a weakness for Sicilian lemons."

"She's seventy-nine, not nineteen," scoffed Monsieur Perrault, unfolding his newspaper. "What's she doing in Italy? Seducing a vineyard owner?"

"Stranger things have happened."

At the butcher's, Monsieur Lavelle said, "Nonsense. She went mad, I tell you. Locked herself in that cottage of hers and forgot how to open the door."

"She's old, not a cat," said Madame Laurent, stuffing a chicken into her basket. "If she got stuck, she'd have found a way out."

At the café, between sips of pastis, Gérard from the post office commented, "Mark my words—she had a secret past. Witness protection. Or a lover in Marseille. Or both."

"A lover?" Marcel, the bartender, laughed. "At her age? The only man she'd be sneaking off with is Saint Peter."

"She was a very spirited woman, Marcel."

"A spirited woman or a woman in spirits, Gérard? She did love a good glass of cognac."

Madame Durant's cottage, now abandoned, became a minor legend. Shutters stayed tightly closed, and the letterbox bulged with official notices, forgotten magazines, and an invitation to a picnic she would never grace.

At parcelle 14 bis, not a single weed appeared. The soil remained healthy, the Saint-Jérôme fern proud. *It's unnatural,* thought Madame Rousseau, cycling by. *A garden left alone should turn to ruin.*

Six months ticked by, the minimum before neglect could be claimed. Then, on a crisp October morning, the trio marched into the allotment office. They were prepared for battle and equipped with patience, determination, and stacks of paperwork. Madame Lemoine, the chief gatekeeper of municipal allotments, awaited them.

Vincent cleared his throat. "We've noticed Madame Durant hasn't attended her allotment for six months," he said.

Madame Lemoine peered over her glasses. "You are Les Trois Pelles, winners for parcelle 14 bis."

"Yes, and we're here to claim it," said Vincent.

"I'm afraid not." She reached for her stamp; the thud sounded final.

"But we won the lottery."

"And your ticket remains valid. However, you may only begin once the plot is officially reassigned."

"And that happens... when?" Pierre asked.

"When the previous holder is legally deceased or declared absent."

"She's missing. It's been six months."

"Yes. Under the Code civil, there must be an official declaration of death or absence, generally ten years after the presumption. If she returns in that time, she keeps the rights. If not, you may petition for the declaration—allow six to twelve months more."

"So, for ten years it just sits?"

"*Les règles sont les règles.*"

Vincent clutched his chest, feeling the first twinge of what would later be diagnosed as allotment-induced hypertension.

Year One: The Optimism of Fools

They sat with their pints at Le Coq Bleu, the local rugby pub, planning their first crops. On the table between them sat a stack of unopened seed packets.

"By this time next year, we would have been harvesting courgettes and tomatoes."

Pierre: "They say tomatoes taste better if you talk to them."

Vincent: "Then Armand's would be doomed."

Armand: "I talk just fine."

"Yes," Pierre agreed. "Like a man giving a halftime speech to a losing rugby team."

They laughed then, naïve and hopeful. By the end of the evening, Armand had placed an order for a handcrafted set of gardening tools. It was never delivered. Pierre noted this was a bad omen.

Year Three: The Denial Stage

They met every Sunday at Café Saint-Rémy, watching the world continue without them. The newspaper lay open on the table.

"Notre-Dame will be fully restored by 2024," Pierre read aloud.

Vincent: "That's only one year before we get our allotment."

Armand: "The French can rebuild a cathedral before we can plant a goddamn carrot."

They started to believe the soil was laughing at their misfortune.

They passed parcelle 14 bis every morning, and there it sat—serene and fertile as ever, basking in its untouchable glory.

Once, Vincent was caught talking to the Saint-Jérôme fern like a spurned lover. "She's waiting for me."

"You need to go on a date," Armand advised.

"I'm in a relationship," Vincent snapped.

Year Five: The Breaking Point

In wine-fuelled desperation one summer afternoon, they approached the mayor's office with an idea.

Pierre cleared his throat. "What if we host a memorial service for Madame Durant?"

The mayor frowned. "But she is not dead."

Vincent clasped his hands solemnly. "Not legally. But spiritually, emotionally—"

"No."

Pierre nodded. "I see. And what if we name a street after her to encourage… closure?"

"No."

"Then, hypothetically speaking, if one were to have a body, but one had misplaced it—"

"No."

Year Seven: The Despair Stage

By now, each of them had aged noticeably.

Vincent's bald spot had spread, a barren patch growing wider each year. Armand's bad leg grew more stubborn. Pierre, once immaculate, now shuffled about in sagging sweaters.

Armand: "What do people even talk about?"

Pierre: "Probably not ten-year land disputes."

"I used to be interesting," Vincent said. "I used to have opinions on things."

Pierre: "You still have opinions, Vincent, mostly about soil pH levels and municipal incompetence."

"I mean opinions that don't make women leave the table."

"You never had those."

Year Nine: The Full Existential Collapse

The municipal office still sent letters to Madame Durant.

"I saw one letter. It was about the upcoming allotment association picnic. She is invited."

"She's dead, Vincent."

Pierre shrugged. "Not legally."

Vincent drained his wine. "If she doesn't RSVP, does that count as proof of death?"

"No."

They stopped trying to argue. The bureaucracy had won.

They faded into the scenery of the town's cafés, nursing espressos and watching fresh faces win and lose the allotment lottery—poor souls still innocent of its curse.

At long last, the time came.

They gathered their papers like soldiers preparing for battle. The ten-year period was over.

Prepared, they marched to the allotment office to claim what was theirs.

Madame Lemoine greeted them with serene indifference. "Ah, gentlemen, I trust you are here to begin the declaration of absence process?"

Vincent's left eye twitched. "Yes—it has been ten years!"

"Oh, yes. But now we must conduct the final legal checks, notify any possible heirs, and ensure that Madame Durant has not been seen within the last… oh, six months. You will receive formal allotment access in approximately twelve to eighteen months."

Pierre snorted through his nose. Armand let out a long, slow sigh. Vincent made a slight choking noise, the bureaucratic equivalent of a pig having its throat slit at the abattoir.

Finally, by spring, parcelle 14 bis belonged to them. They toiled under the sun, planting rows of seeds, dreaming of their harvest.

The Saint-Jérôme fern blackened, its fronds curling inward as if recoiling from unseen blight. A bee, sluggish from the fermented sweetness of flowers elsewhere, dropped lifeless to the ground—an omen the garden bore no innocence. *Digitalis purpurea*, foxglove, sprouted unbidden from the bee's resting place, its scent cloying and stinging the nostrils.

Melissa officinalis, lemon balm, grew twisted and bitter, leaves curling in a feeble protest against the quiet corruption spreading within the soil.

"She cursed it, Pierre."

"Rubbish, Vincent. All we need is chicken and horse shit."

It was the third evening in August when they decided to plant by the moon. The sky was low and swollen. They huddled around an old almanac. Vincent read aloud in his tight accountant's voice, tracing a finger down the smudged print. "Sow root crops when the moon wanes, leafy crops when it waxes. Dig in silence, and let the soil know your breath."

They marked out furrows in the earth with the solemnity of priests preparing an altar. Their spades sliced the soil. Dull thuds. Hoes rasped against pebbles. Forks sank deep, levering up clods that crumbled like stale bread. Armand, sweating under his shirt, pressed bean seeds into the ridges one by one. Pierre scattered a pinch of onion seeds. His undertaker's fingers were delicate, precise. Vincent tamped the soil flat, whispering the calendar's instructions as though each word were a charm.

They stood for a moment, breathing in the damp night air, hands dirty, sweat mingled with loam. The allotment felt unnaturally still, as though waiting.

Then, the earth stirred, a sudden burst of fresh citrus filling the air, a scent so out of place it caused them to look at each other in bewilderment. A tremor ran through the furrows, soft at first, then swelling, shifting, pushing upward. The Saint-Jérôme fern trembled. The ground heaved, cracked open. From the split earth, she rose: Madame Durant, her face smeared with mud, her hair plaited with roots, her eyes glimmering green, the colour of both growth and rot.

"You thought you could take what isn't yours?"

Vincent staggered back. "You… you're gone!"

She smiled, her teeth gleaming like bone. "The soil keeps its own."

Armand was the first to go. The brute of Saint-Jérôme, the man who once ploughed through opponents on the rugby field, thrashed in the grasp of the creeping Saint-Jérôme tendrils, his strength now nothing against the will of the earth. The soil sank beneath him, sucking him down. "No—NO!"

Vincent was next. He tried to run. He tripped on his hoe. The Saint-Jérôme lashed around his throat, tightening, squeezing, sucking him into the earth.

Madame Durant watched.

Pierre was the last.

He did not fight.

He did not run.

He fell to his knees, weeping.

"Please… noooooo."

Madame Durant knelt beside him. "The earth remembers."

Pierre nodded, tears streaking the grime on his face. He reached out, pressing a palm to the soil. The earth shifted beneath him, and he sank without a struggle.

*

Madame Gauthier left the boulangerie with a baguette tucked beneath her arm. It was warm and crisp and would have made a delightful lunch if not for the peculiar business that happened next.

She was halfway home, passing the allotments as she always did, when she noticed a figure on parcelle 14 bis—Madame Durant, kneeling in the soil, pruning something green and leafy. Which was odd. Madame Durant had been gone for over ten years.

Madame Gauthier gripped her baguette. She must have been mistaken. Perhaps it was someone else. No, it was Madame Durant.

"Madame Durant?"

The shears stopped snipping. Madame Durant lifted her head.

Her face was perfectly pleasant, as if nothing at all had happened beneath the soil's surface.

"Ah." She wiped a leaf from her sleeve. "They decided it wasn't for them."

The Saint-Jérôme fern, vibrant and watchful, unfurled its fronds as if in welcome, shadows stretching over fresh, undisturbed earth.

The Man Without a Head

November in London is foggy. On a Saturday morning in 1978, the day before Guy Fawkes, London Bridge stood half-hidden in mist. The world blurred into a grey haze, drizzle not heavy enough to open umbrellas, only soaking the collars of overcoats and dotting puddles across the pavement. Beside his A-board, a vendor bawled, “Daily Star! Daily Star!” Coins chimed in his tin as commuters slid past. Under the red masthead, the board screamed, *CHURCHILL’S CIGAR SOLD FOR £10 IN PUB RAFFLE!*

A crowd shuffled by—some shaking their heads, others grinning at the absurdity of the headline.

A man in a beige raincoat joined the rabble, middle-aged and balding, his briefcase scuffed at the edges. Halfway across the bridge, he stopped—expression vacant—tapping at a packet of Trebor Extra Strong mints.

Out of the fog a naked man came charging, long wild hair plastered to his face, howling nonsense, machete raised. The morning shuffle scattered in every direction—everyone except the man with the mints. He was still shaking at the tube when the machete took his head clean off. It landed with a thud and tipped off the kerb into the river. His briefcase broke open, its contents scattering: a stash of utility bills, cash in coins and notes, a dog-eared copy of *Mayfair* (September 1976, Vol. 11, No. 9), and a cheese-and-pickle sandwich wrapped neatly in waxed paper.

A woman clutched her shopping bag and stumbled back, a jagged wail tearing loose as a cyclist swerved, tyres shrieking, skidding sideways onto the pavement. Another woman fled in panic, her high heel wedged fast in a crack, left behind upright in the pooling blood. The notes fluttered across the pavement; a man snatched one up before bolting. The attacker didn't linger—a flash of machete, his bare back vanishing into the fog, gone as suddenly as he'd come, screaming, "Buckfast, Buckfast! The abbey knows!"

A young constable stumbled forward, pale and unsteady. He bent and vomited across the pavement, choking out, "This… this can't be real." His older colleague barked into the radio for backup. Onlookers crowded close, clutching bags and briefcases, whispering, pointing. A woman sobbed into her sleeve. A man muttered, "Christ almighty… he's still moving."

The rising wail of a siren grew louder—until an ambulance screeched to a halt and paramedics spilled out. Their boots splashed through blood. They froze at the sight of the headless body—"Jesus, he's alive"—before their training took hold. Bags dropped open. Equipment scattered. Their hands worked fast to stabilise what shouldn't have been possible. The body was lifted, strapped, and wired, oxygen forced into lungs as they pushed through the crowd. They shoved the stretcher into the ambulance, slammed the doors, and with sirens climbing and blue lights flaring, tore into the night carrying Leonard Finch—the headless man—toward St Thomas' Hospital.

At St Thomas', the emergency room froze around a sight none of them could explain. The headless body lay on a gurney, chest pumping, limbs jerking in spasms. Doctors clustered close, their voices low. "This is impossible." "Can't be."

By late morning, the case reached Harcourt. He was no surgeon, no physician—more engineer than doctor, known for taking liberties others would not. Where the ward saw horror, he saw possibility.

By mid-afternoon, he had gathered the senior staff in a conference room. "This case," he began, chalk in hand, "is unprecedented. We need to act." He turned to the blackboard and sketched fast: a rough outline of a torso, the spinal cord marked in quick strokes. "Here." He tapped the chalk against the neck stump. "The cord is intact. Signals are still firing." He drew a box above it, with wires branching outward like veins. "With the right neural interface, those signals can be captured… redirected."

The box became a rectangle, a crude television screen. He circled it twice, stepped back, and underlined his point with a single word: *Replace*.

"The head is gone, but the body is still speaking. All we need is to give it a voice."

Silence followed.

Then, "A television?"

"Yes," Harcourt said. "A portable television equipped with processors that can interpret neural signals. The screen becomes his face. The speaker—his identity."

"It's bloody insane. How the hell is this even possible?"

"It's genius. This man… he's alive against all odds. We owe it to him—and science—to figure out how. This man was—still is—Leonard Finch. His voice was the backbone of BBC radio in the fifties. He set the tone with that flawless accent, embodying the authority and trust of public service broadcasting. He was the voice of England."

"How the hell do you know all that?"

Harcourt gave a wry smile. "Check the briefcase. It's all in there."

Some called Harcourt insane. Others, swayed by Harcourt's conviction, saw it as a groundbreaking chance to push the boundaries of medical science.

After fifty-seven minutes of debate, the hospital board approved the procedure. The surgery would last twenty-seven hours.

On the operating table, Leonard Finch's slow, rhythmic breathing continued, steady, oblivious to his missing head.

The shell of a Sony Trinitron KV-9200 television with its nine-inch screen was suspended above his neck. The television had been disassembled, its circuit boards splayed out like the organs of some alien creature. Beneath the screen, Harcourt and his team had arranged a series of processors and neural receivers, each calibrated to translate the electrical signals from the body's spinal column into audiovisual outputs.

The room buzzed with the low hum of machines—oscilloscopes flickered, and heart monitors beeped their mechanical reassurance. A nurse handed Harcourt a soldering iron. He fused the final neural receiver to the spinal cord. "This is the part they'll write about. This is the spark that defies death."

The last connections secured, Harcourt stepped back, wiping his forehead with his coat sleeve. He reached for the activation switch.

"Powering on," he announced.

The television screen flickered to life, its surface first awash with static. The neural receivers whined as they calibrated, their processors struggling to decode the chaotic impulses still firing from the body's spinal column.

The static cleared at a crawl. A face appeared on the television screen—Angela Rippon, with her trademark coiffed hair and unflinching gaze, flickering in the eerie glow of the operating theatre. "Evening," her voice rang out, crisp and steady. "The time is 8:43 p.m., and here is the Nine O'Clock News."

Chairs scraped, a laugh slipped loose, someone muttered, "Christ…"

Harcourt punched the air. "It works. It'll need a few tweaks, but it works."

At the edge of the room, a technician nudged his colleague. "What the fuck have we done?"

Under anaesthetic, their patient was opened at the throat, the oesophagus laid bare. A synthetic ring, cast to measure, was grafted into place—the rim of a new mouth, wide enough for a straw, a tube, whatever he might need to be kept alive. The surgeons stood back, gloves dripping, staring at the body on the table.

Leonard Finch—no longer only a man, now something spliced between flesh and signal—was thrust into the world.

The papers moved first.

THE MAN WITHOUT A HEAD!

FROM HUMAN TO HARDWARE: THE FUTURE OF LIFE?

By Monday the vans were thudding onto kerbs, strewing bundles across pavements; red-tops ran it full-bleed with headlines you could read from a bus, the broadsheets filed grave columns about "the mediated body," and the phone-ins found their callers. By midweek, television schedulers had bitten: an observational series was scheduled twice a week after the late bulletin, working title, *Living Without A Head*—cameras in the flat, a roving unit in the street.

The programme made him legible. Viewers watched Leonard learn about himself on camera. Ask about politics and the set answered in Thatcher's timbre; mention rain and Michael Fish came through the speaker; say "music" and he went to Bowie; say "art" and the KV-9200 dropped into

Picasso. He queued at the post office, took buses, sat in pubs, all while the nation followed. The show needed no plot—only the shock of ordinary life with a television where a face should be.

By the next Saturday, Camden Lock had him pressed and printed. Badge machines clicked out, *NO HEAD, NO PROBLEM.* Iron-on stalls pressed out bootleg tees—a Trinitron for a skull on a suit silhouette with captions like *Live Without A head*, and *No Head No Problem.* Key rings, tea towels, and photocopied fanzine specials cluttered the stall tables.

From a smoke-thick boardroom came the next idea: *Mastermind.*

The studio was shadowed, with the spotlight on an iconic black chair.

"And now," Magnus Magnusson began, his voice crisp and steady, "our next contestant is Leonard Finch—once a familiar voice on radio, later a television personality in the reality show *Living Without a Head*—and, as you can see, literally a man without a head."

Leonard shuffled to the chair, his headless body still unnerving even his most avid fans. The KV-9200 on his shoulders flickered before stabilising into a static, smiling face—a facsimile of a 1970s BBC newsreader.

"Leonard Finch, your general knowledge round begins now. Who was the first President of the United States?"

The face on the KV-9200 morphed to a black-and-white image of a cartoon wig and coat. A stately voice boomed, "George Washington."

"Correct. Which element has the chemical symbol 'O'?"

The Trinitron screen projected a science teacher with glasses and a lab coat. "Oxygen, of course!" came the voice, tinged with condescension.

"Correct."

The audience hushed as Leonard continued his streak of perfect answers. Each response came from a unique character—an explorer answering a geography question, a child reciting nursery rhymes, and a sitcom character offering a punchline-turned-answer.

Leonard finished the general knowledge round without a single error. Magnus Magnusson paused, his face betraying a flicker of disbelief, before turning to the audience.

"Fifteen out of fifteen," he announced. "A perfect score in the general knowledge round. Now, Leonard Finch, your specialist subject: *War and Peace*, the novel by Leo Tolstoy."

The studio lights dimmed. Leonard's screen flickered for a millisecond—a subtle glitch unnoticed by most.

"Your time starts now. Who is the main protagonist of *War and Peace*?"

The screen lit up with the image of a Russian officer, his uniform crisp, and buttons gleaming. "Pierre Bezukhov," the KV-9200 answered with confidence.

"Correct. What is the name of the battle depicted in Book Two?"

The KV-9200 displayed a chaotic battlefield, smoke, and cannon fire swirling as the voice of a general thundered, "The Battle of Austerlitz!"

"Correct."

The questions kept coming, the screen flickering with answers as the clock ran down, until only one remained.

"What is the philosophical essay embedded—" The buzzer sounded, ending the countdown. "I've started, so I'll finish. What is the philosophical essay embedded in the novel's epilogue?"

Leonard Finch appeared on the screen. Not the figure in the black chair, but the man he had been, seated at a BBC radio desk in the 1950s, adjusting the microphone, brow furrowed in concentration. "It's… It's…"

Magnusson shifted. "Leonard? Do you have an answer?"

The screen broke into distorted fuzz. Words formed—

…P..E..A..C..E. WA R. E RRO R.

Magnusson hesitated. "Could you clarify?"

A woman in the audience blurted out, "What the fuck?"

On the KV-9200, a flash-montage burst to life—images crammed into seconds, too fast to hold, too many to process.

A quiz show contestant sweating under studio lights.

A ventriloquist's dummy, lips jerking open.

A test card pattern, with an eye hidden in the noise.

A mouth miming.

The montage cut to a 1969 BBC weather forecast. A calm, smiling presenter, with hair in a neat bob, a floral dress buttoned to the neck. "Light showers expected in the north—"

Her voice cut off mid-syllable. The KV-9200 went dark. Nine long seconds of silence. A chair scraped. Someone coughed. The floor crew stiffened, eyes darting toward the glass booth. In their headsets, the director's voice cracked. "Hold. Hold."

The set fizzed back on. No presenter now, no words—only a single dark eye filling the screen, unblinking, watching everyone in the room. "Peace. War. Peace. War. Peace War Peace, Peace Peace War."

"I… regret to say, Leonard, that is incorrect."

Leonard sat still, the KV-9200 screen now a test pattern. Magnusson shifted in his chair, a hand brushing his earpiece as he caught the signal from the booth. He cleared his throat, shuffling his cards. "And that brings us to the end of tonight's programme. Thank you to our contestants and thank you at home for watching."

The red tally light above the camera blinked out. From the glass booth came the call: "Stand by. Cut transmission." On the floor, the crew moved in, headsets crackling, cables already being coiled.

The audience started trickling out—mutters, nervous laughs. "What the fuck was that?" someone said. Another voiced, "Weirdest thing I've ever seen."

Leonard left the studio, pulling behind him his luggage dolly with a 12-volt lead-acid battery strapped to it: a squat black battery gaffer-taped to a grey inverter, the varnished brick of a transformer stencilled *DO NOT BYPASS*. A mains lead climbed his coat to the Trinitron.

The next day, Leonard sat at his kitchen table, the newspaper in his hands, the blender's whirring a constant soundtrack to his daily beige meal. He flipped past Linda Lusardi on page three, smoothed the paper flat, and stared at the headline.

HEADLESS HORROR ON BBC QUIZ

It was supposed to be highbrow—but turned into a horror show. Millions tuned in to watch Mastermind *last night, only to see "the man without a head", Leonard Finch, sit frozen while his flickering screen spewed bizarre, disturbing images before cutting out altogether. Viewers were left baffled, with one audience member telling us, "I thought it was some sick joke." The BBC refused to comment.*

Leonard read no further. He did not need to. The debacle had left him mocked, turned into a headline instead of a human being. He wanted no part of it. There would be no more interviews, no more panel shows, no more late-night curiosities. He declined every invitation, turned down every offer, and closed the door on the circus.

During this time, solitude became bliss. There were no cameras, no audiences, no questions. Only the kettle, the curtains, and silence.

Over the winter, Leonard sometimes caught himself in the mirror, the Trinitron glowing where his head should be, playing unprompted clips: families laughing at dinner tables, couples dancing beneath string lights, children racing through a park.

Two close friends invited him for drinks at their flat. They ordered sushi from Samurai Joe's and blended Leonard's into a grey slurry. His friends picked neatly at their bright rolls—the pink of salmon, the sharp green of wasabi, the white rice pressed into perfect shapes. Leonard, already practised in the ritual, fidgeted with a clear plastic tube, slotting one end into the opening at his throat and dipping the other into the bowl of colourless sludge. The small pump in his hands gave its low whirr, drawing the liquid through the tube and down into him.

As the last dribbles of the slurry reached the top of the tube, the Trinitron betrayed him.

"So, Leonard—how are things?" one friend asked politely, chopsticks poised.

The screen answered first. A fast-cut barrage of pornographic images—lurid, graphic, relentless—flashed across the screen, then spiral-wiped into a colour test pattern.

An awkward silence followed, then embarrassed laughter. "Looks like an issue with your—its—signal. Is this… you?"

The Trinitron wasn't finished. The test pattern shattered in a smash cut: Hitler's rallies; skeletal bodies in concentration camps; the killing fields of Cambodia, skulls stacked to the horizon; a fly crawling across the eye of a starving child in Biafra.

The screen faded to black.

The malfunctions multiplied.

One day at the corner shop, Leonard overheard a remark about global warming; the Trinitron blinked awake, glaciers collapsing in silence across the screen, ice splintering into the sea. The cashier frowned, then carried on stacking tins. In the supermarket queue, a child tugged at their mother's sleeve, asking about cartoons, and the set answered with a grotesque splice of *The Magic Roundabout* and a World War II newsreel—the jaunty theme bleeding into marching boots and air-raid sirens. The child giggled; the mother pulled her away quickly, avoiding Leonard's gaze.

Late at night, when the flat was still, commercials pushed through unbidden, at first whimsical, then sour. "Careful with that wiring," warned a cartoon electrician, voice pitch-shifted into menace. "Or you'll spark disaster!"

Other times the interruptions were harder to place: a synth chord hanging in the air before being cut short by static; a burst of colour—bright clothes, a white piano, a woman's mouth forming words without sound. Snippets of lyrics floated past him in fragments, broken mid-line: "Pictures… came and broke your… heart." They vanished before he could be sure they'd been there at all.

Leonard began to wonder if the KV-9200 had grown a mind of its own. One sleepless night, the screen filled with a ventriloquist's dummy. Its wooden jaw cracked open. "Who's pulling your strings now?"

On a damp January morning, neighbours reported hearing the same chorus echoing through the walls, played again and again. "Video killed the radio star, video killed the radio star…" It had gone on for hours, maybe days. Officials arrived. The door was forced. Leonard Finch was slumped in his chair, the Trinitron still glowing, the refrain worn down into hiss.

The coroner's report was inconclusive, though Harcourt suspected Leonard had short-circuited the device, ending both the noise and his life.

The funeral was a muted affair. The chapel had seats for twelve. A thirteenth mourner stood outside, smoke drifting from the roll-up in his hand. The coffin lay open at the front.

A local group—The Nutty Knitters—had left their tribute: a hand-stitched cover pulled over the Trinitron, made to look like Leonard's face as it had once appeared on the BBC news, complete with neat parting and a smile sewn in pink yarn. A volunteer from the Bereaved Voices Trust—a thin man in a frayed suit and polished shoes—sang "Abide with Me" in a wavering solo.

Harcourt delivered a short eulogy. The mourners and the priest ambled out of the chapel's yard and across the cobbled path to the Curious Crow, its windows glowing amber in the fog. Inside, pint glasses clinked loudly, the chatter a shade too bright for so few voices.

In 1983, when Hyde Park's peace-festival fringe pulsed with anarcho-punk fury—Crass raging from the stage, The Damned howling into the fog—the soil over Leonard Finch's grave had settled into damp silence, the headstone mottled with mildew.

In the churchyard, a man with long black hair, tangled and unkempt, slumped against the stones, his sleeves darkened with the greasy sheen of bins and hard pavement, coins clinking in his palm as he counted them out one by one. He screwed the lid off a bottle of Buckfast. He tipped his head back, took a swallow, and blinked at the headstone facing him, its face mottled with mildew. He squinted, leaned close, traced the letters with a dirty finger, and read aloud in a slurred half-sing.

"Here lies Leonard Finch. 1924–1980. A man without a head. But not without questions."

He snorted, took another sip. "Headless man, eh? Who'd have known…" A cough rattled in his chest, and around him the last of the autumn leaves stuck damp to the stones, winter pressing close.

Appendix: Razorblade Fanzine (Issue 7, 1980)

TV FOR A HEAD / DEAD INSIDE

London fog + Buckfast bloodbath + BBC brain-drain = The Man Without a Head.

Some commuter loses his noggin on the bridge, yeah? Some clever doc bolts a SONY TRINITRON where his skull should be.

Zap zap, wires + flesh, flicker flicker, signal screams. LEONARD FINCH: ex-BBC voice of calm, now walking advert break.

Q about politics = Thatcher sneer.
Q about weather = Fish says drizzle.
Q about life = static static static.

It's Frankenstein in colour, LIVE on the Six O'Clock News.
Mastermind meltdown—test card turns to eye turns to WAR turns to PEACE turns to ERROR ERROR ERROR.
The nation laughs, pukes, tunes in again.

This story ain't horror, it's biography.

We've ALL got a telly for a head.

We've ALL swallowed the adverts, the quiz shows, the headlines.
Leonard just made it visible.

Best bit = the funeral.

Knitters stitch him a face, BBC smile in PINK YARN.

Dead man, static screen, sewn grin.

COFFIN HUMS, CROWD STARES, HEADLINE LIVES.

READ THIS IF YOU THINK YOUR TELLY ISN'T WATCHING YOU.

READ THIS IF YOU THINK YOU STILL HAVE A HEAD.

The Miracle of Moira

The year was 1986, when Northern Ireland wore two faces: one scarred by checkpoints and headlines, the other green and timeless as pasture. Between border tension and bomb scares, there was one week each May when the island pretended to be whole again.

It was time for the Balmoral Show. Farmers arrived, tractors gleaming, pulling prized livestock. Stalls brimmed with local treasures—jars of marmalade, fresh soda bread, and rounds of cheese wrapped in linen.

This year's show was special, as Queen Elizabeth and Prince Philip attended. Union Jacks fluttered, and the pavilion was decorated in the pastel colours favoured by the monarch.

The Queen emerged from the car, a vision of elegance in her cornflower-blue coat and matching hat. "It's a fine turnout."

"Indeed." Philip smiled wryly. "Though I daresay the cows look cleaner than the farmers."

However, the true heart of the Balmoral Show wasn't in the royal pavilion or the food stalls; it was in the show ring, where generations of hard work and careful breeding clashed in fierce competition. Among the dairy-cow entries was Moira, the champion Friesian owned by Samuel "Sammy" McQuillan, a Protestant farmer from the borderlands of South Armagh's "Bandit Country".

Sammy had spent the early morning hours in Moira's stall, brushing her flank. "It's not just a show, girl—it's pride, it's heritage." Moira had twice won Best of Breed and Best Milk Yield, and today she looked poised to take the title for an unprecedented third time.

Judging began, led by a renowned Yorkshireman. He circled Moira, examining her balanced frame and symmetrical udders, while junior judges nodded.

The crowd jostled. "That's McQuillan's cow—she'll be the one to beat."

From her seat, the Queen observed, "That's a remarkable creature." She tilted her head towards Moira.

Prince Philip jibed, "Nearly as polished as the farmer's head."

The results were announced. Moira was indeed crowned Best of Breed and Best Milk Yield for the third consecutive year. Sammy tipped his cap to the crowd and Her Majesty.

As the sun set, Sammy led Moira to her trailer. The trophy sat beside him for the ride home.

It started later that evening, as most strange things do.

The victory called for a proper celebration, and Sammy, like any self-respecting farmer, didn't believe in half-measures. By midnight, the whiskey bottle was half-empty, and Sammy was swaying in his chair, mumbling words of gratitude to the only creature he trusted: Moira.

With one boot only just clinging on and the other missing, Sammy staggered toward the shed, the bottle and trophy in hand. Moonlight glinted off Moira's medals hanging from the beams.

"Three bloody years, girl!" Sammy slurred, his voice bouncing off the corrugated roof. "Yer milk's pure gold! And what do I get? A bald head and a farm no one gives a shite about. But you—yer a queen, Moira. A bloody queen!"

Moira, chewing in her stall, turned her head toward him with calm, dark eyes that said, "Yes, I know, I am magnificent."

"Yer better than the lot o' them, y'know that?" Sammy slumped against the barn door. "Don't care for borders, do ye? No bombs, no feckin' politics—just milk and ribbons. That's how it should be."

He dropped the trophy. As he bent over to pick it up, his sweat-soaked cap slipped off and landed in the straw.

"Ah, Jaysus," Sammy groaned, bending to retrieve it. As he reached, Moira dipped her head, and her tongue extended, giving his scalp an unexpectedly deliberate, lingering lick—far more attentive than her usual nuzzles, as if bestowing a strange blessing.

Sammy froze. His whiskey-soaked brain struggled to process what had just happened.

"What the feck?" He wiped his scalp with his sleeve. "Moira! Ye big eejit! Ye think I'm a salt-lick or somethin'?"

He chuckled, shaking his head. "Well, good on ye, girl. Yer a better conversationalist than most o' the folk round here."

Satisfied with his congratulations, Sammy staggered back to the house, none the wiser that Moira's slobbery affection had just changed his life forever.

The next morning, Sammy woke with a pounding headache and a maddening itch on his scalp—right where Moira had licked him the night before. He stumbled into the bathroom. "What the hell's this now?" he muttered, squinting at the cracked mirror. His hand froze mid-scratch. There, scattered across his once barren scalp, was stubble—tiny black dots sprouting like seedlings in tilled soil.

"Sweet feckin' Lord." Sammy leaned closer, shocked. "Is this real? Am I growin' hair or goin' feckin' mad?" He glanced back, remembering Moira's tongue on his scalp.

By the second morning, the stubble had thickened, and by the end of the week, Sammy's head was crowned with a lush, curly mane, as black and shiny as a peat bog after rain. He stood before the mirror, running his fingers through. "Look at me. I look like a young Sean Connery. Feck, Moira, what've ye done to me?"

Eager to test the waters, Sammy donned his cleanest shirt and boots and strode into the Crossmaglen pub, where his bald head had been a familiar sight for decades.

He pushed open the door, and the chatter died away. Heads turned, pint glasses paused mid-air, and disbelief spread through the room.

"McQuillan!" roared Charlie the barman. "What the feck's happened to yer head? Have ye been rollin' in Miracle-Gro?"

Sammy grinned, striding to the bar like a man half his age. "No Miracle-Gro, Charlie. It's all mine."

"Mine, my arse!" barked Big Gerry, a farmer with hands like spades. "Ye've been bald as a billiard ball since before I could shave! What's yer secret? Witchcraft?"

Sammy tapped the bar for a pint. "It was Moira."

"Moira?" Charlie frowned. "Yer cow?"

"Aye," Sammy replied. "She licked me head after the show. Next thing ye know…" He gestured at his curls. "This."

The room erupted in laughter. "Go on outta that, Sammy!" shouted one man. "Next ye'll be tellin' us she can fix the gearbox on me tractor with a sneeze!"

Sammy raised his pint with a grin. "Laugh all ye like, lads. The proof's on me head."

By the next morning, word of Sammy's miracle cow had spread like wildfire across South Armagh. Bald men from every corner of the parish—and some from beyond—turned up at Sammy's farm, clutching caps in hand and hope in their hearts.

"Alright, McQuillan," said Seamus Donnelly, a retired teacher. "I don't know if yer takin' the piss, but I'll pay good money to find out."

Sammy folded his arms, pretending to consider. "Alright, Seamus. Sixty quid. Moira doesn't work for free." The men in the queue started pulling out their wallets, counting money.

Moira was tethered to the farm gate as bald men queued down the lane, each clutching £60. One by one, they bowed before Moira, offering their shiny heads to the cow. Unbothered by the fuss, Moira delivered her licks with calm precision, her wide tongue leaving a damp streak and a faint tingle of hope. As the line grew longer, a lone voice from the crowd called out, "That cow's tongue is worth more than my herd!"

By the end of the week, the first success stories began to emerge. Men returned to the farm, pulling off their caps to reveal tufts of fresh growth.

"Look at this!" cried Jimmy McKenna, the butcher. "It's comin' in thick as feckin' brambles!"

The farm became a sensation, drawing visitors from Belfast, Dublin, and beyond. Cars clogged the roads as Moira's fame spread.

Observing the chaos from his gate and feeling the cash in his pocket, Sammy said aloud, "Bandit Country, my arse. This is Hair Country now."

The phenomenon demanded attention. The first sniff of the story came to Jimmy Brogan, a chain-smoking reporter for the *Newry Gazette*, who'd made a career out of covering stories no one else wanted to touch. With his scuffed shoes and nicotine-stained fingers, Jimmy had an instinct for the absurd, and when he heard rumours about a cow in South Armagh licking bald men back to hairiness, he knew he'd struck gold.

Jimmy observed the men at the gate of Sammy McQuillan's farm, waiting for their turn with Moira's miraculous tongue.

He scribbled in his battered notebook, trying not to laugh at the sight of their shining heads glistening in the sun.

"You're tellin' me," he said, puffing on a bent cigarette, "that this cow—this actual, honest-to-God cow—is growin' hair on scalps like she's feckin' magic?"

"I'm not tellin' you, Jimmy. I'm showin' ye. Look at me head!" Sammy pointed to his lush black curls. "If it weren't for Moira, I'd still be bald as a feckin' egg."

Back in the newsroom, Jimmy typed it up with a grin on his face, adding just the right mix of disbelief and drama. The next morning, the *Newry Gazette* hit the stands with a headline that blared from the page: *McQuillan's Golden Cow Cures Baldness!*

The article became the talk of South Armagh. Farmers chuckled into their porridge, priests raised eyebrows, and barbers across the region cursed. The tale might have lingered as a local curiosity if it hadn't reached Brussels.

Dermot O'Reilly, a well-known Member of the European Parliament, read about Moira while sipping his morning espresso in his Brussels office. Dermot's hair situation had been the subject of snickers for years. His colleagues called him "The Flying Carpet"—a nickname that stung as much as it stuck.

His thinning hair reflected mockingly back at him in his desk's polished surface as he picked up the phone and connected to his secretary. "Book me a flight to Belfast.

There's an agricultural phenomenon requires immediate investigation."

The next morning, Dermot arrived at Sammy McQuillan's farm in a government-issued car, his entourage in tow. Dressed in a sharp grey suit and carrying a leather briefcase, Dermot claimed he was there to "inspect cross-border agricultural policies". But within ten minutes, he had discarded the briefcase, loosened his tie, and joined the queue of bald men.

Dermot's turn came; Moira sensed the moment, her large brown eyes fixed on the sweating politician as he knelt before her. With one tongue sweep, she delivered her trademark lick, leaving a damp streak of saliva across Dermot's shining scalp.

By the end of the week, his head was crowned with a luxurious mane of auburn hair. He called a press conference. Cameras flashed as reporters jostled for the best angle. Looking ten years younger and at least twenty pounds lighter, Dermot raised his hands in triumph. "This cow is not just an Irish treasure but a European one! Her gift must be shared with the world."

The story went international overnight. News outlets across Europe picked up the tale:

Wunderkuh heilt Glatze in Europa!

Bovine irlandaise remonte le temps!

De Bruselas a Belfast: un fenómeno peludo!

Men began arriving from Amsterdam and Antwerp, clogging the narrow roads of South Armagh with sleek

European cars. Sammy raised his prices to £200 a lick, and the line grew. Moira, ever the professional, carried on her work with the same calm dignity that had won her ribbons at Balmoral.

Across the channel, inside De Gouden Koe—"The Golden Cow"—Marie-Claire De Vries, the leader of the Ardennes Front for Liberation and Progress, sat at the head of a battered oak table. A Gauloises cigarette dangled from her lips. Around the table sat half a dozen members of the Front.

She tapped the table with a crumpled newspaper. "Gentlemen, what you are about to hear will change everything."

Thierry, a wiry man with a moustache thinner than a sweep of eyeliner, asked, "What is it this time? Another shipment of potatoes to Luxembourg?"

Marie-Claire exhaled a cloud of smoke. "No, Thierry. This"—she jabbed at the newspaper headline—"is far more lucrative. So shut up and listen. Merde!" She read aloud, "'Irish Farmer's Cow Cures Baldness'! Did you get that, Thierry?"

"A cow? This must be a joke."

"Do I look like I'm joking? Men are queuing in South Armagh, paying obscene prices to have their bald heads licked. And what does that mean, gentlemen?"

"Bacteria?" Geert offered.

"It means money. More than we'll ever see smuggling rifles to those morons in Luxembourg. If we steal the cow, bring her here, and charge €2000 a lick, Europe's vainest men will fund our revolution and make our cause unstoppable. Do you understand, Thierry?"

"But how do we move a cow across borders? This isn't our usual smuggling gig, Marie-Claire."

"We will rely on our comrades in Ireland."

The group readied for action. Soon, their plan was playing out on a misty, bone-chilling night in South Armagh.

The McQuillan farm lay still. In the distance, an owl hooted. Three figures emerged from the shadows.

Paddy "Shovel" O'Loughlin lifted a finger to his lips. "Keep it quiet, ye gobshites. We're professionals."

Behind him, Seán "Chisel" McGrath tripped over a loose plank, sending a tin bucket clanging across the yard. He gritted his teeth; stealing a cow felt beneath him, but the promise of a payday—and the odd thrill—had pulled him along. A startled chicken squawked as it flapped into the rafters.

Inside the barn, Moira stood calmly in her stall. She turned her head as the men entered.

The trio approached cautiously. Seán slipped a halter around Moira's neck, giving it a gentle tug.

"Pull harder," Paddy said.

"She's heavier than a tractor!" Seán grunted.

"She's just stubborn. She needs… encouragement."

"What kind of encouragement?" Declan "Half Pint" Murphy asked.

"Cows like music. My da used to say so."

"Music? We're not runnin' a bloody céilí!"

But Paddy was already humming "Danny Boy". Declan joined in. Soon, all three sang, their voices echoing through the barn.

Moira let out a long, disapproving moo.

In the farmhouse, Sammy McQuillan stirred, his sleep ambushed by the wild chorus. He grabbed his shotgun and stormed into the barn. "What in the name of Jaysus…?"

He halted, taking in the bizarre tableau: three grown men, red-faced and desperate, crooning "Danny Boy" to Moira.

"WHAT IN GOD'S NAME ARE YE DOIN' WI' MY COW?!"

Paddy shouted, "RUN!"

Sammy raised his shotgun, firing a warning shot into the air. "GET OFF ME LAND, YE EEJITS!" As they scarpered, he shook his head. "Bloody eejits. They don't make thieves like they used to."

Back in Antwerp afterwards, Marie-Claire, cigarette in hand and frustrated, addressed the Front in the backroom of De Gouden Koe.

"Last week's attempt was a disaster. A 'Danny Boy' serenade? My God, even Belgian cows would have resisted. We have a satellite video call with the Irish about their failure."

On the screen, three men in knitted tricolour balaclavas stared back, their sheepish eyes peeking through the wool like schoolboys being scolded by a terrifying nun.

"This is your final chance," she told them, "and here are some clues… tranquiliser darts, a stolen milk truck, and—listen carefully this time—some competence. Get. The. Cow."

On the screen, one of the balaclava-clad trio said, "Right. Competence. Got it."

A few days later, they free-wheeled a truck, lights off, through the gate of the farm and pulled up outside the barn. Inside, Moira munched on hay.

Declan raised the tranquiliser gun and pulled the trigger. The dart hit Moira in the flank. She blinked once, let out a soft, questioning moo, and collapsed into the straw.

"She's down! Get the winch!"

The trio sprang into action. They winched, heaved, and shoved Moira's hefty frame onto the truck. "This is goin' too smoothly, boys…"

The barn doors crashed open. Framed by swirling fog, Sammy McQuillan stood there, shotgun raised. "NOT MY FECKIN' COW!" he bellowed.

Paddy tackled Sammy, sending the shotgun skittering across the floor. They rolled through the straw, limbs flailing wildly as they exchanged increasingly creative curses. Sammy got Paddy in a headlock.

Seán, standing a few feet away with the tranquiliser gun, panicked. "Hold still, Paddy! I'll take him down!"

"DON'T SHOOT!" Paddy screamed, escaping Sammy's grip.

The dart embedded in Paddy's arse.

"Ye… feckin'… eejit…" Paddy slurred, toppling onto Sammy.

"GET HIM OFF ME!" Sammy roared, his voice muffled beneath Paddy's bulk.

Declan fired a second dart that hit Sammy as he staggered to his feet, his face twisted in fury and confusion. "What… in the name of… feckin'…" he mumbled, weaving unsteadily, and with that, he toppled face-first into the straw.

Seán and Declan hauled Paddy's unconscious body toward the milk truck. Declan clambered into the driver's seat, his fingers fumbling with the ignition. The truck lurched forward, its wheels skidding on the frosty ground.

Declan glanced nervously back at the barn in the rearview mirror. "Is he followin' us?"

Seán twisted around to look. Sammy lay sprawled in the straw.

The milk truck rattled through the countryside. In the back, Moira stirred.

*

MIRACLE COW KIDNAPPED IN MIDNIGHT RAID

Sammy McQuillan vows vengeance after beloved bovine vanishes

By Mairead Mallon | Staff Reporter

Outrage swept South Armagh yesterday following the brazen abduction of Moira, the prize-winning Friesian cow famed for her alleged hair-restoring powers.

Moira, who has gained local and international notoriety after reportedly curing baldness with a single lick, was stolen in the early hours from the McQuillan farm.

"They broke the gate clean off its hinges," said owner Samuel "Sammy" McQuillan, visibly shaken. "They led her away like common rustlers. Except this isn't common—this is feckin' sacrilege."

Authorities confirmed hoofprints, drag marks and tyre tracks at the scene. Constable Sheila Bogsworth said the perpetrators "knew exactly what they were doing", citing evidence of tranquilliser use.

"This wasn't a prank," she added. "They weren't after beef. They were after the miracle."

As word spread, locals flocked to the farm. By dusk, more than two hundred people had gathered at the fence with candles, thermoses, and tribute items: ribbons in county colours, faded photographs, and tufts of freshly regrown hair tied with string.

The most striking moment came after sunset, when a dozen previously bald men formed a silent circle around Moira's empty stall. Each removed his cap and placed a lock of hair into a brass bucket once used for her feed.

"She gave us back more than follicles," said Seamus Donnelly, a retired teacher and one of the first recipients of a "miracle lick". "She gave us dignity. She made us believe again—in something larger. In the power of cows. In small miracles that smell of silage."

The photograph on the front page of the paper—candles flickering against the weathered barn, the bald men kneeling in reverence—was taken by local teen Aisling Maguire, who said she hadn't seen her da cry like that since the Pope came to Drogheda.

Standing alone at the broken gate with a length of Moira's halter ribbon clutched in his hand, Sammy spoke only once at the impromptu vigil. His voice was thick with grief but steady.

"I'll find her—I'll find my girl."

*

Moira's kidnappers reached Belgium; the truck wheezed to a halt outside a large farm. A sign on the gate read: *PRIVATE PROPERTY – RETREAT IN SESSION.*

Marie-Claire stood at the barn. "I see you brought her alive, Paddy."

"What did ye expect, minced meat?"

A bespoke yurt was erected on the property, imported from Mongolia but refurbished in Bruges with Belgian hardwood floors, silk wall linings, and underfloor heating. At the heart of the room stood Moira. She wore a ceremonial silk halter embroidered with the word *Believe.*

They came from everywhere, slipping past borders and bureaucracy with desperation in their eyes and cash in their suitcases. One Saudi prince arrived beneath a diamond-encrusted head covering, a decades-old bald spot hidden beneath layers of royal linen and hope. A Hungarian general followed, solemn-faced and sweating gently, muttering in his native tongue that the sacred cow had come to him first in a childhood dream. Even a UK Cabinet Minister was rumoured to have made a late-night visit, returning to Westminster two days later with a thick, suspiciously lustrous fringe and a new lease on political charisma.

Those lucky enough to be licked were issued an embroidered silk scarf embossed with a cow's head emblem inside a mandala.

Marie-Claire called it "the Protocol". She recited the rules like gospel before each session: "These are the rules. No cameras. No tape recorders. No refunds. And, above all, you tell no one who licked you."

Security was absolute. Thierry employed former Swiss guards and one man who claimed to be ex-KGB, though he mostly attempted newspaper crosswords at the front gate.

It was a Wednesday. The client sat in the back of a blacked-out Audi, scalp still glistening. He stared turned on his portable recorder and held it to his mouth. "It was… warm. Like the breath of God… I saw things. My childhood. My first wife. A three-legged fox… I've had stem cell injections. Laser hats. But this? This was real. I came here bald. I'm leaving changed. She is not a cow. She is a presence."

The chauffeur tilted his hat. The car pulled away. Inside, the client wept silently into his scarf.

Seán Brannigan was an investigative journalist, though tonight he wore the skin of Dr Declan Faraday, Personal Follicular Advisor to the Sultan of Oman. The disguise was outlandish but plausible enough.

He arrived at the gates of the retreat in a rented Citroën, driven by Joost, the Belgian fixer who had delivered more than one journalist to the fringes of madness.

A woman was waiting. "Welcome." She knelt before him, carefully untying his shoes. His brogues were placed in a velvet-lined casket marked "Surrender." Then came the blindfold, cool silk tied slowly around his head. She adjusted the knot. He was turned gently and guided forward. He was brought to his knees on a cushion.

And then—without fanfare, without flourish—came the lick.

Warm. Slow. Ceremonial.

Then it was over.

Back in the Citroën, Brannigan's fingers shook as he retrieved the mini camera that had been hidden in his jacket lapel. He plugged it into the laptop balanced across his knees. Her face filled the frame. Breath fogged the lens. And then, slowly, reverently, her tongue reached forward and delivered the holy stroke.

"Sweet Mother of Hair," Seán whispered. "It's her. Moira. The Crossmaglen Cow." He turned to Joost. "They've got her. She's here. Licking heads in a yurt in the woods of Wallonia. And I swear to God… I think I've got a fringe."

FRINGE BENEFITS AT €10K A LICK

Seán Brannigan uncovers international bovine black market deep in the Belgian forest

Byline: Seán Brannigan, Investigations Correspondent, Private Eye

Excerpt:

Readers may remember Moira, the so-called "miracle cow" from Crossmaglen, who once licked a pensioner's bald patch into something approaching a thatch. Well, she's back—only this time she's not grazing in South Armagh. She's in the Ardennes, moonlighting as the follicular Messiah of Europe's elite.

What I witnessed in a candlelit yurt in Wallonia was equal parts Lourdes, livestock mart, and dodgy barber's back room. Bald men shuffled forward on their knees, blindfolds tied tight, waiting for their bovine blessing. And lo, the holy lick was duly administered, with all the pomp of a handshake at Davos.

Behind it all stands one Marie-Claire De Vries, self-styled revolutionary and full-time opportunist, who has apparently decided that armed struggle is passé and that the real money lies in dairy-based quackery. Her organisation, the grandly titled Ardennes Front for Liberation and Progress, is less Red Brigade, more red rags and milk pails.

To be clear, this isn't a health spa, it's an international bovine black market. A clandestine lick-for-cash racket in which the going rate for a head-swipe from Moira is rumoured to start at €10,000, rising steeply for repeat customers or those with particularly stubborn crowns. Baldness, it seems, is the final frontier of desperation.

In summary, the cow is real, the miracle is real, and the scam is very real indeed. Whether the world's powerful emerge with thicker hair or merely thinner wallets remains, like Moira herself, something of a mystery.

Within hours, questions were raised in Stormont. Northern Irish ministers demanded action.

"We want our cow returned," roared DUP MLA Malcolm Spratt. "She's a national treasure, not some continental hair therapist!"

Sinn Féin released a statement: "Moira belongs not to the powerful, but to the people. Her tongue is a symbol of unity. And milk."

The UK Home Secretary called for "immediate extradition of the bovine in question".

The Taoiseach remained silent, though he was seen reading *Private Eye* with a grave expression and an uncharacteristically thick fringe of hair.

Marie-Claire De Vries held a press conference outside De Gouden Koe. Flanked by her lieutenants and a life-sized portrait of Moira in ceremonial harness, she addressed the world from behind a curtain of smoke and contempt.

"We will not surrender Moira to capitalist nations that exploit beasts and barbers alike. Moira will be returned when the British government releases all political prisoners aligned with the Ardennes Front for Liberation and Progress. And," she added coldly, "we want a year's supply of Barrys Tea."

Reporters stared, stunned.

Weeks passed. Headlines flourished. Protests erupted.

In the end, it wasn't threats or tribunals that resolved the crisis, but a quiet sequence of back-channel negotiations conducted far from microphones and headlines. The talks involved, among others, a weary UN agricultural attaché with a fondness for oat biscuits; a goat-whisperer from Monaghan named Philomena, whose powers of persuasion were said to rival her livestock's instincts; and, most curiously, a handwritten letter from Daniel O'Donnell—unexpectedly moving, immaculately polite, and oddly effective in shifting the mood of the Belgian delegation: *I write with the deepest respect to ask that you consider the people of Crossmaglen, for whom this cow is more than livestock. She is part of their story, and I believe kindness can carry further than any border.*

Between them, through soft diplomacy and sheer rural determination, a deal was struck. In exchange for the quiet release of seven extremely elderly and largely forgotten political prisoners, the return of one antique Land Rover, and ten boxes of Barry's Tea, Moira would be released into Irish custody under veterinary escort.

It was a Friday of rare sunshine when Moira returned to Crossmaglen. The bunting, which had gone up the night before in a rush of string and staples, fluttered between buildings like the town had been gift-wrapped. The kazoos were already tuned, and the local accordionist, Mickie Dolan, had polished his buttons to a shine not seen since his niece's confirmation.

Moira's float arrived just past midday, turning onto the main road with a gentle lurch that made her bells jangle in dignified protest. She was standing regally, if slightly bored, atop a custom-built cart shaped like a golden udder. Behind her trailed a choir of twenty bald men in ceremonial sashes, walking two abreast and carrying long beeswax candles that occasionally dripped hot wax onto their hands. They hummed as they walked.

Children waved paper cow masks on sticks, most of which were upside down, and a woman from the ladies' committee passed out "miracle milk fudge" wrapped in Moira-embossed foil. Near the community hall, a local artisan had set up a stall selling keepsakes, including holy water bottles labelled "Moira's Moisture" (filled with Ballygowan), and a commemorative calendar with twelve glamour shots of Moira in various pastoral poses.

There was a short ceremony in the square. The crowd hushed as Sammy stepped up to the microphone. "She's been to Europe and back." He paused. "She's licked princes, ministers, generals, and desperate men. But she never forgot her roots. She never once said she was too good for the field, the frost, or the company of ordinary folk. And I'll tell you this now—she's no one's bloody shampoo mascot. She's a queen. A Crossmaglen queen."

The crowd erupted. Bunting fluttered. Someone shouted, "Viva Moira." A child cried, though that was possibly due to the taste of the vegetable sausage roll his father had just handed him by mistake.

Moira blinked—slowly, wisely—acknowledging the praise while wishing everyone would just calm down so she could return to the shed and lie down for a bit.

Later, when the kazoos fell quiet and the rain stilled the bunting, Sammy sat in the barn beside Moira, nursing the bottom of a bottle of Bushmills.

"Well, girl," he slurred, "you've done what no pope or politicians ever managed—you've united this town with nothing but a tongue and a bit of grace."

The wind picked up hard and flung the barn door open. A startled rooster hopped, flapped, squawked, and somehow landed on the antique rifle that had hung above the feed sacks for years. The rifle slipped, butt-first, bounced once off the sack of silage, and discharged—a single shot ricocheting off the enamel bathtub full of rainwater and catching Moira above her heart.

The vet came. Then the council. Then the forms were signed.

There were no speeches. No bunting.

She was taken—quietly, respectfully—to McKenna & Sons Meat Processing, a long low building outside Armagh where animals met their end with a mix of indifference and bureaucracy. They logged her as "Friesian, adult, deceased," and she entered the system like any other beast, though the lads in the back did notice that she had a certain presence, even on the hook.

Nothing was wasted. Within a day, they used it all. Her sirloin went to butchers, her mince to supermarket lasagnes, her bones to broth, and her offal into pies—dozens of pies.

One particular batch—labelled *Local Beef & Ale, 3 Dozen, Distribution Route C (Pub Trade)*—was wrapped, boxed, and delivered to five small establishments across the province.

Another impromptu vigil took place.

The choir of men arrived first. They came at dusk, heads uncovered despite the drizzle, each carrying a single beeswax candle and a folded handkerchief stitched with her name.

They gathered outside the barn. Some knelt. One sang. Local children placed offerings: tufts of hair, a cowbell wrapped in tinsel, one glitter-glued shoebox with the words *Thank you, Moira* in rainbow letters. An old man stood silently, clutching a sausage roll like a crucifix.

Seamus Donnelly addressed the mourners. "She was more than a cow. She was a kind of peace treaty. A creature that asked for nothing, gave everything, and licked without judgement."

Sammy said nothing. He sat inside the barn, in her empty stall, a cup of cold tea on the straw beside him, staring at the halter still hanging from the hook. The ribbon, though weathered, held its colour.

Three weeks on, with memories of Moira still fresh in conversation, Aidan O'Hare ducked into the Crooked Colt for warmth, shelter, and a hot meal.

He was a simple man. Tired, damp, and grateful to be out of the wind. He asked what was hot. The barman pointed to the pie oven. "Local beef. Hot enough to burn your tongue and rich enough to make you forgive your da."

Aidan ate every bite. Flaky pastry. Peppery gravy. He wiped the crumbs from his shirt and said aloud to no one in particular, "That's the best pie I've had since my wedding."

That night, he didn't sleep. By morning, he was hallucinating about sheep with sunglasses and claimed to hear Gregorian chants from his toaster.

At the hospital, the diagnosis was a shrug dressed as Latin: "Some kind of encephalopathy."

The news broke in whispers—first heard in barbershops and bus shelters, repeated across fences, mentioned with unease between pints. Another man in Ballynahinch had also fallen ill after a pie. They said it was serious.

And then someone at the Department for Food Safety made the connection—the delivery date, the route, the batch. It all pointed back to one cow, one moment, one bullet. Moira.

MIRACLE COW BECOMES NATIONAL THREAT

WAS HAIR LOSS CURE WORTH IT?

LICKED BY THE BEAST?

Experts argued over ethics, oversight, food safety, and sainthood. A local councillor proposed banning cows from licking anything without a government-issued licence. There was talk of a public inquiry.

But none of it stuck. Because something had happened. Something had passed between Moira and the people—something bigger than rules, risks, meat pies, and madness. She had made them feel seen. She had given them back something they hadn't known was missing: dignity, hope, the strange and beautiful possibility that life might surprise them again.

In the spring, a statue went up in the park beside the stream, funded by donations in envelopes scrawled with notes like, *For the miracle*, *She saved my marriage*, and *Because I haven't worn a hat in months.* It was nine feet tall, cast in bronze, its tongue extended in a gesture both absurd and holy.

A song was written and banned from RTÉ for being "lyrically confusing and spiritually ambiguous".

Pilgrims came quietly. A man from Donegal swore his psoriasis cleared after stroking the statue's hoof. Another man left a single pie on the plinth every Sunday until a dog stole it and was later found with unusually glossy fur.

The field where she once grazed was renamed Lick Vale.

And in the quiet corners of barbershops and barrooms, people still spoke her name—not loudly, not sentimentally, but with the warm grin of those who knew they had once lived in the time of Moira.

Statue Inscription – Lick Vale, Crossmaglen

MOIRA

Queen of Cows. Licker of Heads. Healer of Hair.

1979–1986

"She never judged a man by his politics, his past, or his pate—only by whether he stood still and let her do the job."

Funded by the grateful, the balding, and the bewildered.

The Tuesday and Thursday Club

It all began on a Tuesday.

Thandi stopped at the gate and checked her phone: 78A, St Peter's Road. She pushed open the low iron gate and climbed the three steps to the front door. On either side, rose bushes stood bare, the hips holding the last orange of the year.

An envelope with a message scrawled on it was taped to the front door: *If you're from the agency, come in. The door is open.*

Thandi rapped lightly before stepping inside. "Mrs Pritchard? Hello. I'm Thandi. Thandi Mhlanga, from the agency."

Joyce looked up from her armchair, tea-towel across her lap, Sudoku book balanced on it, fountain pen in hand. A wheeled walker leaned against the armchair.

Books filled the sitting room. Six bowed bookcases lined the walls, and smaller towers leaned in corners—behind doors, on the piano, beside the bed. There were hundreds, more than a lifetime of reading. In the kitchen, the kettle on the Aga rattled its lid; the volume of *Woman's Hour* was turned down.

"You'd better come in," Joyce said. "And close the door—the draught is merciless."

Thandi set her bag by the umbrella stand and unwound her scarf, ID badge knocking against her tunic. At the bottom of her bag, a notebook bound shut with elastic kept poems she had never shown a soul.

Joyce smiled. "Before we start, let's make tea and have a little chat. Remind me of your name again?"

"Thandi Mhlanga."

"Mshlanga?"

"Close. Thandi is fine."

They sat at the kitchen table with cups of milky tea. By the kettle, Thandi noticed a thin book leant against the biscuit tin.

She looked through the window at the back garden—slightly larger than the front—where November showed only remains of summer's foliage, stems brown and bowed. A robin hopped on the feeder at the windowsill, its breast bright in the grey.

"When robins appear, loved ones are near," Joyce said matter-of-factly, watching the bird.

"Ooooh... In my country we say if a bird comes to your home, it carries news from the ancestors. Sometimes good, sometimes not. But always worth listening."

The robin stopped feeding and gazed at the activity in the kitchen.

"Where are you from?"

"Bulawayo. Zimbabwe."

"Bulawayo," Joyce repeated. "My husband was with the BSAP—the police—back in the sixties, during all that trouble... the Bush War and such. Terrible business. Pity, really, about the farms—the whites, you know..." Her voice faded.

Thandi smiled, a little embarrassed. "My grandfather was with the church then. My father worked in the mines. It was a long time ago."

"Right, let's talk work. I have a list." Joyce pointed to the mantel. "Over there. Next to the mantel clock."

Thandi picked up the list. Beside it sat a birthday card, open. A child's handwriting inside read, *Happy 83rd Granny, from all of us in Australia xxxxxx.*

She turned her attention to the list:

- bathroom tiles—scrub any mould from the grouting (stubborn as sin)
- picture frames—dust and straighten (especially the one of Whitby)
- freezer stew—three tubs at the back, defrost one for Thursday supper
- plants—water, not too much water, especially the African violet
- robin feeder topped up (watch him, greedy little landlord)
- torch batteries (check drawer, traitors hide there)
- dust piano keys, but don't play
- keep biscuit tin full—custard creams if possible
- spare hot-water bottle under bed—don't move it
- gas meter reading (note down, man never trusts me)

- check postbox—ignore leaflets, bin them straight away
- torch by bedside in case of power cuts

On the second Thursday, the robin pecked at the food Thandi had just replaced. Joyce gestured at the sink unit. "That's where the traitors live."

Thandi opened the cupboard. Inside, pots and pans tangled in a friendly chaos, lids perched askew, trays wedged at odd angles, stray utensils hiding at the bottom.

"You keep everything."

"Redemption is always possible."

Thandi crouched at the cupboard, moving the contents into some kind of order. She gathered the pots, stacked the lids, eased trays back where they belonged, and settled the jumble bit by bit. She looked over her shoulder at Joyce. "What do you think?"

"Better than I've seen it in years. Thank you."

Their time was up. Thandi wound her scarf about her neck, pausing in the hall. "I should mention, Mrs Pritchard, next Thursday I may be late. I have to go to Lunar House in Croydon, for my visa. Is that okay?"

By the following Tuesday, as winter's chill crept in, the space between them had softened. Pauses settled comfortably; silences lost their stiffness. Thandi dusted a bookshelf with gentle care, her yellow cloth gliding over poetry, gravy-stained cookbooks, and a shoebox of yellowing

Penguin novels tucked beneath the spare chair. Joyce watched her work.

"You're careful. You're not like the others. My books don't like to be disturbed. They sulk, but they outlast everyone. Better than people. Never betray you. Never steal the biscuits."

On the fourth Thursday, Thandi tapped the front door politely before entering 78A. She shook the damp from her coat. Joyce was at the kitchen table, the day's list half-finished in front of her, the pen laid across it. Beside it lay her crossword book, *The Times Quick*, open to a page abandoned mid-clue.

"You'll have noticed the place is a clutter. I've decided it needs clearing. Everything. The lot."

"You have many books. Should I start there?"

"No, no, no. Not the books. They're not books. They're my friends."

The words hung between them like commandments.

"Then I'll leave them," Thandi said finally. "I'll start with your cupboards."

After that, the questions changed.

Joyce leaned back in her chair, glasses low on her nose. "Enough about flights and fares. Tell me—what are you reading?"

"At the moment? A little Dambudzo Marechera. He doesn't behave, but I like him."

Joyce smiled. "A poet worth his biscuits, then. And which line won't leave you alone?"

Thandi looked to the window. "'I am the stone that breaks all your knives.'" She gave a small shrug. "It stays even when I don't want it to."

"And do you write?"

Thandi nodded, a touch embarrassed. "Sometimes. Slowly. A sentence is like a bird—it escapes if you grip too tightly."

"Good. That's how it should be. Look here—my lists have started misbehaving."

She passed the list to Thandi. Between cleaning the bathroom tiles and not disposing of torch batteries in the recycling bin, a thin line had crept in: *Violet on the sill, forgive me.*

Thandi traced it with her finger, smiling. "Even your chores are learning poetry. My mother used to sing to potatoes while peeling them. She said it made the skins fall easier, like forgiveness coming off in strips. In Shona we say '*Rwiyo runorodza mwoyo*'—a song soothes the heart. Even the potatoes listened."

"Thandi, do you write?"

Thandi excused herself to get her notebook from her bag. She sat, opened the notebook and began to read.

friendship is a road without tarmac,
it remembers every step,
dust rising soft as prayer.

in Bulawayo we said **hama***,*
kin, not only of blood but of spirit—
to call someone hama was to shelter them.

one day the jacaranda will flower again,
lavender rain across the pavements,
and we will walk there together,
even if our bodies have forgotten how.

Joyce listened as Thandi spoke, her face entirely given to the sound. Then she slid a book across the table—the one that lived by the biscuit tin. "I keep this one close. For fortification."

Thandi opened the book. The pages were filled with lines, quotes, poems, and small sketches. She flipped to the last page. She read aloud, her voice steady in the small kitchen.

the heart is old ground
yet still it waits for rain

Joyce nodded. "That one kept me upright more than once."

On subsequent Tuesdays and Thursdays, routines shifted, and they often skipped cleaning. Instead, they moved to the kitchen table near the Aga, letting conversation become their habit.

They talked and read. They read Simon Armitage for his modern take on ordinary lives. They read Larkin for his ordinariness. They read Gabriel García Márquez for magical memory. They read Monica Ali for city life and new beginnings. They took turns reading. One found the page, the other chose a line. They sometimes argued about punctuation.

A good visit included three passages, laughter, and pencil marks. The robin stayed at its feeder. The house got used to their voices. The days passed. Outside, neighbours strung Christmas lights, mocking the darkness. Thandi opened day 14 on the advent calendar propped on the kitchen table beside *The Grass is Singing.*

"You've read this one?" Joyce asked her. "Lessing. First book of hers I ever bought. Colonial Rhodesia. Bleak, sharp as a thorn."

"We read her at school in Bulawayo. She wrote about home, but not in the way we knew it."

Joyce reached for Thandi's hand and gripped it firmly. "Please stay the night," she said. Her voice was softer than Thandi had ever heard it, a child's request slipped from an old throat.

Thandi hesitated. "I shouldn't. It goes against the rules."

"No one will know. Not the agency, not anyone. Just me. Just stay."

Thandi looked at her, saw the plea behind the insistence, and nodded. "Alright. But first I need to fetch something from the shops."

The tram hummed through the December dark, and Thandi returned with a bag heavy on her shoulder. Inside was maize meal, a bundle of greens, a packet of peanuts, onions, and a small tray of chicken thighs.

Back in the kitchen, she set water to boil, ground the roasted peanuts with the pestle Joyce kept for herbs, and stirred them into a bubbling stew of onions, tomatoes, and greens. The smell of peanut butter thickening into sauce filled the air, nutty and warm. She fried the chicken with garlic until the skin crisped, added it to the pot, then set another pan on the stove.

"This," Thandi said, stirring the second pot, "is sadza. Our staple. It takes strength to stir—my grandmother always said you have to beat it until it stands by itself."

Joyce watched as the maize meal thickened into a dense white mound. "Proper food," she said, "solid, no nonsense. Just looking at it makes me feel full."

They ate together at the table by the Aga, steam rising from bowls.

Joyce lifted a spoonful, chewed slowly, then closed her eyes. "Nutty, earthy—it sits on the tongue like a good poem."

"Back home," Thandi said, "we eat it with our hands. You roll the sadza, dip, and scoop. But I think we'll use spoons tonight."

Joyce laughed, and for a moment she looked younger, less wintered. "Spoilsport," she said, dipping her spoon again.

Afterwards, Thandi washed the dishes, stacked them neatly, then spread a duvet across the sofa in the sitting room. The books towered around her like quiet companions, their spines catching the firelight. She lay back, listening to the tick of the mantel clock before falling asleep.

*

A week before Christmas, on the Thursday, tram 2553 was crammed with Christmas shoppers. Thandi carried a parcel of her own, tied with string, with a sprig of rosemary slipped beneath the knot. Inside was Tsitsi Dangarembga's *Nervous Conditions*, its cover soft from other hands. On the title page she had written: *For Joyce—because girls must always find their voices. Xx Thandi.*

The flat at 78A St Peter's Road smelled of lavender. Joyce sat in her chair as always, with the tea-towel folded, the walking frame beside her. The garden glittered with frost; the robin chirped.

"I'm here," Thandi said. "It's only me." She gently set the book on Joyce's lap and then made tea.

On the mantel beside the list was an envelope addressed, *Thandi.* The card inside was simple—a robin and holly on the front cover—and inside were the words, *Thandi, Merry Christmas. Friends do not end; they shelve themselves inside you. Love, Joyce.*

Outside, a child dragged a sledge along the dry pavement and invented snow with his voice. The radio announced carol service times.

Thandi wrote on the mantel list with Joyce's fountain pen: *Thursday—dusted, watered, soup in fridge, robin insolent. African violet is blooming. Much love x T.*

She touched the back of Joyce's hand, then pulled on her parka and stepped into the cold. Tram 2553 stopped at East Croydon for her.

The World According to Danny

Who the fuck wants to be called Danny?

Not me. Never me. You spend your whole life dragged around by a name someone else slapped on you, like a price tag that won't peel off. Danny. It makes people think I'm some builder's sidekick or the kind of bloke who bellows at football matches. But that's not who I am.

I'm more like a Wolfhound–collie cross with a nose for rain and a knack for philosophy. I'd have chosen something older, something with teeth—Bran, maybe, or Cúchulainn if you're feeling dramatic. Instead I get Danny. Two syllables shouted across fields, slurred when he's had a whiskey too many.

Don't get me wrong. I've heard worse. A mate of mine at the park—Staffie-Jack Russell mix—got called Mr Pickles. Imagine living with that. You'd chew through your own lead.

Anyway, dignity matters. These days I prefer the fire. The warmth gets into me and holds me together. Outside, the Welsh wind flattens the grass and scares the crows out of the trees. In here, by the fire, the world almost makes sense, and I can rest a moment from everything aching outside.

Walks? Forget it. He still tries, the old man. Jiggles the lead like it's a holy relic, calls me Danny in that sing-song voice, as if I've forgotten who I am. I humour him sometimes, limp down the lane, sniff at a post. But truth is, I'd rather stay by the fire. The body's not built for marathons anymore.

Still, when I do go out on his lead, I make it worthwhile. Nothing better than dropping a steaming coil right where it's hardest to scoop. Watching him bend, bag in hand, face twisted, muttering curses—that's poetry. My kind of poetry. Small victories, you know? Once I crapped in a clump of stinging nettles.

Food's another farce. Wet muck from tins. *Grain-free. Vet-approved. Beef flavour*—though I've never met the cow it came from. He sets it down like it's a gift from the fucking gods. I eat because I must. But don't think I don't compare it to better things. And yes—licking my own balls is one of them. Don't look at me like that. You've never tasted dog food.

He thinks if he buys the *premium* blend it'll trick my nose. Mate, I've smelled your socks. Nothing about you says "salmon". Give me the pan scrapings, the roast grease, the toast that fell butter-side down. I've eaten fox shit and called it a delicacy.

Evenings stretch. He sits in his chair, eyes glued to that box with colours. Crime shows, cooking shows, some braying panel of faces arguing about nothing. And he thinks I'm the dumb one. I watch him watching, and I wonder: Is this what being human amounts to? Sitting, staring, waiting for something to change?

They call it "the shelter", and sometimes "the rescue". I guess it makes humans feel saintly.

I was there, sure—concrete pens, a line of us pretending not to need anyone, tails banging metal. A woman with a clipboard looked at my teeth and called me a crossbreed like I didn't already know. Irish Wolfhound and Border collie.

I suppose I'd better tell you how I ended up here with the old man. It's a long road from shelter to firelight. Before the shelter, there was Haze. Not his real name. Close enough. You know the type: long straggly hair that smelled like a forgotten laundry basket, music vibrating through my paws at two a.m., spliffs rolled fat as thumbs that left a burnt earthy smell lingering in the air, smoke thick as curtains. The ash got into everything, leaving a bitter taste on my tongue. He rolled his afternoons into paper and forgot to roll me into his life. Sometimes he loved me hard, his face pressed into my neck, his breath humid, eyes wet with promises. Other times the door stayed open, the fridge empty, and I learned to lap up stale water from a plant pot. The soft *click* of a lighter flicking in the dark became a night song, one that spelled solitude.

When I chewed the corner of the sofa and littered the alleyway with plastic and vinyl-encased crap, the neighbours called the council. I was lying on the floor chewing bits of carpet. A woman with soft hands and a firm voice took me out, and his voice—from the mattress—said, "It's chill, he's chill."

So yes, shelter. The metal pen. The echoing barks. The hopefuls and the hopeless. I settled into the rhythm—eat, sleep, listen, pretend. I worked out which volunteers smelled of meat and which of guilt, and which were vegan. Eventually

I learned to sit for the ones with clipboards. A week passed. Two. Dogs went out and never came back. Good for them.

He arrived on a Saturday. Hands too big for his pockets. Trying to look like someone who knows what to do with grief. The manager said he'd "recently lost his wife", like loss is a thing that happens once and then stops. He looked at me. I looked at him. Neither of us made a connection. I definitely didn't choose him. I didn't choose anyone. He said, "Danny?" at random, as if the name might fit. The clipboard woman beamed like a midwife. I went home with him in a car that smelled of damp blankets and Dettol. It could have been stale human piss—I'm not sure.

I need to tell you about our walks. They always ask on walks, "Is he a rescue?" As if I'm the poster child for their goodness. As if my face is a test they can pass with a biscuit. I give them the stare: the long, slow, "mind your business" stare. He apologises for me. "He's shy," he says, which is a polite way of saying I don't trust people who announce their kindness to strangers.

Then the chorus: "Awww, he's lovely, isn't he?"

Am I?

Am I your idea of lovely in your shiny coat and your pocket treats and your voice like a baby's?

"Can I pat him?" No. "Does he sit?" Sometimes. "What mix is he?" A mistake with legs. "Irish Wolfhound and collie? That's interesting." Interesting is what humans say when they don't know what else to say. I sniff their shoes and file them under harmless but noisy.

One afternoon a child asked, "What's his real name?" I nearly respected that.

He said, "Danny," gently.

"His real name," the child insisted.

He looked down at me. I looked back. A wind came over the hill and pressed our clothes and fur in the same direction. He said, "Bran, maybe," and the child nodded, satisfied, and we both accepted the lie that felt truer than the truth.

The vet calls me an "older gentleman." As if that's meant to soften the thermometer up my arse. I stand there, tail at half-mast, while she pokes and prods and gives him that look—the pitying one, like she's already written my obituary. He nods, mutters "Yes, of course", and pockets the pills he'll forget to hide in cheese. I don't complain. Complaining gets you sympathy, and sympathy gets you another jab.

Then there was last winter.

A catalogue came through the letterbox. One of those things aimed at older humans. Full of adverts for slippers with memory foam, trousers with forgiving waistbands, bath rails shaped like swans, garden hose extensions. That sort of thing. He must've been in one of his moods—soft around the edges—because next thing I know, he's ordering me a "premium canine thermal bodysuit". Waterproof. Windproof. Dignity-proof (not).

It took him eleven minutes to get it on me. I resisted for every one of them—not out of drama, but principle. But then he sniffed. His eyes went glassy. A strand of snot hung from his nose like a surrender flag. So, I relented. Not because he'd won—never that—but because pity trumps pride.

So, there I was. Trudging down the lane in a bright-red Lycra disgrace, snug in all the wrong places, emblazoned with the words *Arsenal Forever*.

Of course, the neighbours were out. The jogger with the spaniel paused mid-stride. The woman with the labradoodle giggled behind her scarf. A child pointed and whispered, "Mummy, is that dog in fancy dress?" in a voice loud enough to shame a foghorn.

Back home, he peeled it off gently. Folded it like it was the flag of a fallen soldier. Laid it on the radiator to dry. I lay by the fire licking (or was it gnawing?) my front paw for half an hour. Not because it needed cleaning, just because it was the only part of me that hadn't been violated by polyester.

I never saw the suit again. Maybe he buried it. Maybe it climbed into the bin of its own accord. Either way, we never spoke of it.

And that in itself was love. Thank fuck.

Then there's that bloody yellow budgie—Pretty Boy. Headbutts the bell and the mirror in his cage all day: *clang, chirp, clang, chirp*. Keeps shrieking, "Who's a pretty boy then?" I'm convinced he's brain-damaged. Punch-drunk. You can't bounce off your own reflection that many times and come out sane.

And the old man talks to him like he's the bloody Pope.

"Morning, Pretty Boy. Want some fresh air?"

Sometimes he (the old man, not the yellow budgie) talks to the empty chair. Mentions "Margaret" a lot. Not loud, just his lips moving. He doesn't notice that I hear. I always hear.

Dogs are archivists. We file everything: tone, gesture, silence. I file the way he says her name as if it might keep her seat warm. On some days when we walk, we stop at a stone in the yard next to the chapel. Here he murmurs her name softly. His eyes tear up.

When he coughs in the morning, I pretend not to notice. He pretends it didn't happen. We are both liars in our own ways.

And still, the walks.

Jingle-jangle of the lead, voice pitched high. "Danny, come on, boy!"

I sigh, shuffle, humour him. Out on the lane, the same questions, the same hands, the same bloody chorus: "Is he a rescue?" Yes. Always yes. Nobody asks the better question: What did you rescue him from?

Some days I dream of running. Hills wide open, sheep scattering, tongue loose, air sharp. I wake to my hips creaking, fire low, his hand twitching in sleep. Dreams outrun us, but we keep chasing anyway.

One day, I'll stop dreaming.

He'll stop coughing.

And then what?

They'll call me a rescue again. They'll put me in a car that smells of Dettol and damp blankets and baby shit. They'll give me another name, maybe softer this time, Buddy or Alfie. I'll stare them down.

What will they expect of me? Sit vigil by the chair? Fetch the paper and pretend it matters? Fuck that. I'll do what I've always done: watch, wait, file the moment. Add it to the archive. I'll answer to none of it. Because I am not Danny. Not Bran. No rescue.

I am the fire's warmth, the shit in the nettles, the silence beside a man who pretends the cough means nothing.

And that's enough.

If I ever write a book—call it a dog's guide to (mis)understanding humans, or just an autobiography with teeth—I'd put that on the back cover: *I am the fire's warmth, the shit in the nettles, the silence beside a man who pretends the cough means nothing.*

Perhaps the publisher will title it *The World According to Danny.*

He's thinner this winter.

I can sense it in his cheekbones when I nose him awake. He folds blankets with unnecessary care, lines up mugs like soldiers. Little signs.

The neighbours hover. One brings soup, another bread. The last one with the red hair smells of pity. He thanks them, sets it all down, forgets to eat half. I nudge a bowl now and then—not out of hunger, just to remind him he's still here.

He coughs more. Pretends less. Sometimes we don't walk at all. He rattles the lead, laughs at himself, and sits back down. We sit together, staring at the box when it's on, at the fire when it isn't. He tells me I'm a "good boy" in a voice that sounds like an apology.

The last morning is bright and sharp, with frost on the sill. He calls me close. His hand rests heavy on my head. We stay like that for a long time. Then he whispers the word "walk" almost as a joke, and I think—what do you want me to do, take you for a walk?

I don't move. I've learned the power of staying still.

He breathes slowly, slower, stops.

The room doesn't change, but everything in it tilts.

The kettle hisses. The clock ticks. The fire pops. I file it all away.

The neighbour comes later. Soft voice, blanket, the whole routine. I lie where I am, between the chair and the hearth. She steps over me carefully. She calls me "poor Danny". I don't bother correcting her. She calls the men in uniforms who bring an empty stretcher.

That night I walk to the door and sit. She figures it out eventually. We go out into the cold. The lane is empty. The chapel stone waits, name rubbed smooth. I stand there for a while, like he always did. Then I lift my leg, leave my line in the frost, and head home.

Back inside, the fire glows. I curl myself close, paws stiff, nose tucked. I dream of hills, sheep scattering, my name carried by the wind—not Danny, never Danny, something older, something with teeth.

If there's another walk waiting, I'll take it when I'm ready. Lead or no lead.

My pace. My path.

Good lad.

The World According to Pretty Boy

They sit there like a bloody Rembrandt for Depressives.

Him in the chair, telly glowing blue on his sagging face, probably watching some BBC4 bollocks about medieval doorknobs. Or worse, *Antiques Roadshow* with that woman—the one who smiles like she's just smelled a corpse in a doily.

Once, he whispered "Margaret" during a segment on commemorative biscuit tins. Just sat there, eyes glassy, muttering her name like the ghost of a custard cream might bring her back.

Pathetic.

And the dog—Danny.

Curled up by the fire like he invented suffering. Farts so toxic I'm convinced he's trying to gaslight the room.

He gives the old man that look—the soft, sad, shaggy, "I get you" look.

Please. He's just cold and too lazy to die.

Fuck them.

He gets the fire. He gets the floor. He gets the silence and the sighs and the blanket of shared misery like it's some sacred fucking ritual.

And me?

I get the cage. The fucking bell. The reflection of my own perfection bouncing back at me like a punchline with no audience…

Anna And The Tree

Part I – The Measure of Things

Tharandt Forest, Kingdom of Saxony, Autumn 1821

The forest corps arrived with tools slung like rifles: callipers, brass chains, compasses. Officers and cadets—men of the Royal Saxon Corps of Forest Surveyors, trained at Tharandt. Their task was clear: map the forest into obedience. They would classify. They would tally. They would prepare it for a future shaped by yield.

They moved in pairs and trios through the forest, speaking of volume, stand, crown density, yields, and succession. Chalk marked bark. Theodolites clicked. Young men in crisp green coats crouched beside trunks, fingers blackened with graphite and larch sap as they measured diameters, density, span.

Anna Wiegand stood just beyond grid N8, at the edge of section 8B. Sketchbook open, pencil resting against her glove. She had been sent to assist Herr Volkmann, her father's former pupil, now a senior in the Royal Forestry Corps. Before his death three years earlier, Johann Wiegand had served as chief surveyor to the Saxon Crown—a man who taught his daughter to measure rivers and mountains with the same precision he once demanded of cadets measuring trees. She sketched crown spreads and diameters, annotated species in a tidy hand. Her presence was tolerated so long as her lines stayed straight and her tongue still.

Then she saw it.

A beech—*Fagus sylvatica.* Not the tallest, nor the widest. Its bark, usually smooth ash-grey, was mottled and green-veined, darkened in places like weathered marble.

In the old poems her father read aloud, the beech was a tree of silence and longing. A keeper of lovers' initials, unsent letters. In Saxon folklore, it cradled sorrow in its bark and never split in a storm. Some called it the widow's tree. Others, the listener. Her father called it the tree that remembered what others tried to forget.

Anna stepped toward it. Twenty-three paces from the survey line, beyond the reach of record. She brushed her fingers along its flank. The bark felt warm, welcoming.

She closed the sketchbook, ran the pencil tip once across her lower lip, and slipped it into her apron pocket. "I will return."

She carried the tree's warmth as she walked home.

That evening, she sat with her mother at the kitchen table. The faint scratch of needle kept time beside the hiss of the lamp. The survey ledger lay open beside the sewing basket. Anna reached for her pencil to record the crown spread from section 8B. Instead, she sketched—wide curves at the base, tapering upward and parting slightly down the centre. She added folds from memory—a soft cleft, a second ridge, that faint asymmetry her fingers had traced more than once in the comfort of her bed.

She stared at it: her sex, drawn in full. She tore the page from the ledger, folded it once, pressed it to her mouth, kissed it, and tucked it into the lining of her dress.

She woke twice in the night—first from a dream of sap running up her legs like stockings, and later simply to stare at her palm, where bark had once touched her and left no trace.

Part II – Return

Tharandt Forest, Autumn 1821

She waited three nights, each one tighter than the last—lying quietly beneath heavy covers, fists pressed to her thighs, breath held. At first, she swore she could outlast it, clinging to resolve. By the fourth, desire had taken root. It was no longer a thought.

She left just after supper, telling her mother she carried a meal to the gravedigger's widow. She left the bundle at the church steps.

Anna took the long way round, avoiding the dirt track used by the forestry corps. She followed the deer path on the ridge instead. The moon hung waxen and near, peering between the trees.

She reached section 8B. The forest lay silent. She turned, counted—twenty-three paces—and stopped.

The beech seemed to tilt toward her, its bent trunk inviting. She stepped into the clearing and exhaled slowly.

Kneeling at its cradle, her skirt pooled around her. She drew the small leather notebook she had once used to chart her father's river bends and opened it to a blank page.

She wrote;

"I spread my skirts
to the ground
and kneel
sunk
before you
you find
the seam—
the wet line
where hunger
has no language
only
rhythm"

Her cheeks warmed, a blush pressing hard against her skin. She traced the grain of the bark, feeling fissures like lines of verse etched into the wood. She leaned her cheek to the cool trunk. In the quiet, she felt a soft thrumming deep inside her, like a familiar caress.

When she opened her eyes, the moon had shifted. Her pulse slowed; her thighs still tingled where they had pressed against the tree. Rising unsteadily, she smoothed her skirt and held the notebook to her chest.

"I know what you are," she whispered. Then she slipped back into the forest.

The next day, Anna helped update section 7A's timber records with Herr Volkmann, nodding at the proper moments, drawing and writing in neat, quiet lines.

That evening she sat by the hearth. Her mother's needles barely moved; the yarn drooped loose in her lap. Anna wrote:

"i press my thighs
against you
bite down
on the wanting
let it swell
let it wet
let it ache
where no one sees
but me"

She closed her eyes, then wrote some more:

"i rot
sweet
at your root
ripen
without shame
until nothing
inside me
stays whole"

She closed the book and kissed its cover gently.

Part III – The Roots

Tharandt Forest, Late Autumn 1821

By the time the leaves turned the colour of old bruises, Anna could no longer sleep without first feeling the tree against her in her mind. She no longer measured time in meals or bells but by absence—how many days since her body had fitted in the cradle between the roots.

She went back that evening.

She knelt before the tree, her skirt bunched unevenly, one stocking damp from a patch of moss she hadn't noticed. Her brow grazed the trunk; one hand touched the bark above her head.

She let the weight of the day fall away.

She slid a hand beneath her skirt.

Her fingers began to move.

She made no sound, only opened her mouth—slack, wet. Then it came: a sudden tightening, her body locking, mind splintering beneath the surges and releases. When it passed, she sank against the trunk.

From her coat she drew the notebook, fingers still damp from moss and wet, and wrote:

"i kneel until my knees are slick with moss
and heat
you fill my space
i stay open

long after you are
done with me. "

Part IV – The Interruption

Tharandt Forest, November 1821

The leaves had thinned. The bark darkened with rain.

Anna had begun to leave gifts: a strip of pear skin, the tip of a graphite pencil, a curl snipped from the nape of her neck. She buried them near the roots, pressing the soil down with bare hands. She wrote lines that came unbidden.

Some nights she didn't write.

Some nights she simply sat with her skirts hiked up, thighs chilled by the bark's kiss, letting her breath fog the damp air.

So when she heard the snap of a twig behind her, it didn't register at first as danger.

She stood too quickly, yanked from her private world. Disoriented and anxious, she pulled her skirts down and grabbed her notebook. The interruption left her exposed, her connection to the tree severed too soon.

"Fräulein Wiegand?"

The voice was bright, casual—laced with arrogance.

She turned.

Cadet Elias Schönfeld stepped from the gloom. His uniform was neat; his cheeks flushed from exertion—or excitement.

"Out for a sketch?" His eyes dropped to her hem, her bodice, her waist.

"I heard a rustle," he added. "Thought perhaps a deer had wandered from the herd. But no. Just you."

He sniffed once and wrinkled his nose.

"What is this place?"

He took a step forward. "Strange tree," he said. "Crooked. Like it's praying. Like it wants something."

Anna moved to step around him, but he caught her wrist.

"Wait. I've not finished asking."

Her notebook fell.

It landed open on the moss. They both stared at it.

She bent to retrieve it. He dropped to his knees and snatched it before her hands reached.

He turned the pages. His lips moved silently. Then aloud: "Your hollow took me."

A half-laugh, half-scoff escaped him. He turned another page.

"*I bloom at your base*—These are… obscene. Poems to a tree? You're mad."

Anna didn't move.

He was close now. "You should be punished for this. These poems—they're evidence. Of madness. Of sin." His voice dropped. "And if I don't report them…"

His hand moved toward her waist.

Anna didn't flinch. "Touch me, and the tree will know. It will remember. And what grows from that memory will find you."

"Witch," he muttered, and fled, clutching Anna's book pressed to his chest.

Interlude: Trial Fragment

Royal Forestry District Court, December 1821

MAGISTRATE: The court shall now hear evidence regarding the seized materials. These were recovered from the possession of Cadet Schönfeld on the evening of November 12th and consist of thirteen handwritten pages of verse.

SCRIBE: Shall I read them aloud, Your Honour?

MAGISTRATE: No. Let their titles suffice. *The Hollow. Bloom. Sap Prayer. Between Root and Crown.*

PASTOR BLEICHER: The girl is unwell—and dangerous. There is no repentance in her writing, only glory in decay.

MAGISTRATE: Let the record show that the accused was found alone, in possession of indecent verse, in proximity to Crown-protected forestry stock. She has refused to renounce the writings or explain their content in Christian terms.

ANNA: I do not speak Christian terms.

MAGISTRATE: That much is clear.

Part V – The Trial

Royal Forestry District Court

Tharandt, December 1821

The courtroom was built of pine. Its windows were narrow. The magistrate's robes were stiff with starch; his mouth was pinched.

Anna Wiegand stood chained.

MAGISTRATE: Fräulein Wiegand, you are aware of the charges brought against you?

ANNA: I am.

MAGISTRATE: Do you contest the authenticity of these verses?

ANNA: No.

MAGISTRATE: They are yours?

ANNA: As much as they are anyone's.

He sighed.

MAGISTRATE: We are not here to dance with metaphor. These are not hymns. They are—let me not understate—lewd, pagan, and dangerous.

He glanced at one page.

"No man has ever kissed me the way the hollow took me"

He snapped it shut.

PASTOR BLEICHER: I have read the entire collection. Not once is the Almighty invoked. There is no repentance—only craving. Filth dressed in rhythm. This is not poetry; it is worship of decay.

MAGISTRATE: Of a tree, no less.

ANNA *(softly)*: It was not just a tree.

MAGISTRATE: Then what was it?

ANNA: It was the only thing in that forest that did not lie.

Memory: The Last Visit

She went once more after the poems were taken from her. It was three nights before they came for her.

Snow had come early, lying in soft drifts between the roots. She pressed herself against the tree.

It was the first time she wept beneath the tree.

Back in Court

MAGISTRATE: You say this was a private matter, yet your writings were found in public space—read by a Crown cadet, recorded, transcribed.

ANNA: Stolen.

MAGISTRATE: Regardless. The content speaks for itself: *I bloom at your base. Sap between my thighs.* These are not reflections of a moral woman.

ANNA: You do not want a moral woman. You want a silent one.

MAGISTRATE: You wrote of your own body as if it were a forest.

ANNA: It is.

The magistrate set the pages aside. The pastor shifted, his face red. The door opened briefly to admit more townspeople.

MAGISTRATE: Let it be known that the accused refuses to recant. Her writings are heretical; her conduct indecent. She is to be confined to the Magdalenenheim of Hellerau for correction. Her materials are to be destroyed. The specimen—the tree—is marked for controlled felling.

ANNA: You cannot cut what is already inside me.

MAGISTRATE: What did you say?

ANNA: Cut it down, burn it, grind it to paper—I will still bleed green when you strike me.

Part VI – The Sanction

Hellerau, Spring 1822

Inside the Magdalenenheim, the windows were narrow and high, admitting thin slices of light. Women moved quietly here, some with eyes downcast, some wide open, seeing only what they refused to name.

They had burnt her poems, cut her hair. What remained was coiled at the nape of her neck. Each morning, she braided what little was left: left braid for root, right for crown, centre for hollow.

She was allowed to walk in the garden. She walked barefoot. She loved that.

It was the day before the solstice. Her hair had grown. She rose early, before the nurses started their duties, before the other women stirred beneath woollen covers and prayed. It was the morning of the monthly inspection when the guards gathered in the director's office and the garden door stood unwatched. She'd noticed the gap weeks ago. She slipped through barefoot and didn't look back.

She reached the clearing as the light began to bend—pale gold on green, shadows long and soft as silk. The beech was waiting. She undressed slowly, each piece of cloth folded and placed on the earth. Then she stood naked in the hush, hair loose.

She stepped forward, pressed her chest to the trunk, her hips settling where the tree dipped. Her fingers traced the grain that had opened her.

And she spoke her final poem.

"they burned my words

cut my hair

locked me in rooms with God

but you remained in my mouth

my thighs

the wet dark

they couldn't reach

i am here to make good

on my promise

when i first knelt

call it rot

call it ruin

i call it home. "

She kissed the trunk, one slow press of her lips, and her poem ended. Her mouth came away wet with sap.

She tasted it. Swallowed.

Then Anna curled at the tree's cradle, knees to chest, hair fanned like roots, breath slowing until it ceased.

By morning, a dark stain had spread across the moss as if the tree had wept her into its roots.

Autumn 1823

It had been marked for removal—its lean deemed irregular, its growth unproductive—but the report was misfiled, the marker faded, other priorities intervened. The axe was delayed by a clerk's error—paperwork outlasting flesh. The tree remained.

*

Early Spring 2025

Tharandt Forest

The walk was meant to clear her head—too many hours at the screen, too many notifications. Her AirPods played something ambient. A city girl visiting cousins, she followed the trail app.

Her phone buzzed in her pocket like a trapped bee. She stepped off the path to read the message.

The beech was there beside her: crooked, leaning slightly, moss climbing one side. She paused her music, pocketed the AirPods.

She walked up to the beech and laid her hand on its bark. It was warm.

Slowly, she lowered herself to the ground, cross-legged, back leaning against the trunk.

From her bag she took a small notebook and a pencil. She opened to a blank page and began to write:

”you leant
as if remembering
what it meant
to be wanted slowly
without reply
i opened my legs
like an answer
i didn't mean
to say aloud. "

Author's Note

The events of *Anna and the Tree* are set in 1821, during a formative moment in environmental history. That same year, in the forests of Saxony, Germany, Heinrich Cotta and the Royal Saxon Forestry Corps were laying the early foundations of sustainable forestry.

While not the first forest survey in Europe, it was among the earliest attempts to measure, map, and manage a forest as a renewable resource using scientific principles—a radical shift from centuries of extraction and improvisation.

Tharandt, where this story is set, soon became home to one of the first forestry academies in the world. It was here that concepts like *Normalwald*—the "regulated forest"—were developed, forming the roots of what we now call sustainability.

This story imagines a quiet resistance within that moment.

The Nineteenth That Never Was

Dennis sits at his desk, Metallica in the background—"For Whom the Bell Tolls" shaking the cheap speakers. He pulls the battered jotter closer, lined A4, corners bent, cover curled like old bread. The Parker pen uncaps with a click. A bead of ink trembles at the nib. He sips from a half-tin of beer, warm and metallic, and turns the volume up.

First word goes down heavy, gouged in black: ***NINETEENTH.*** A circle around it. A star. Underline.

An arrow out, jagged. *Needs hook. Short story? Poem? Both?* The ink smudges beneath his thumb.

Klaus lands on the keyboard, screen flashing gibberish. Dennis pushes him off and the cat sulks, tail twitching on the radiator.

Next scrawl: ***HOUSE.*** Circle. Arrow. *Curtains drowned in the river. Panes trembling though no wind moves. Names hover, waiting to be spoken. Never mine.*

A branch taps the windowpane. Dennis looks up. The koi pond glints black in the night. A fin flicks, circle widening, gone. He lowers his head, pen scratches again.

STAMP. Double underline. *Gum sharp as iron. Envelope thirsty. Tongue stings, copper ghosting the mouth.*

Beer sip. Bitter. Another ring stains the desk.

Margin scrawl: ***CHILD.*** Star beside it. *Smile too old. Film grain thickens. Frame hums like a funeral bell.* Crossed out *Child.* Replaced with *Boy.*

Ink spiral. Pen coughs, blotting the corner.

QUARRY. Asterisk. *Black water breathing. Reeds bending. Covenant sealed. Ripples only.*

Klaus yowls, claws the air, then settles. Metallica's riff rattles the window glass.

THORNS. *Roses opening darker than sleep. Petals cling, fingertips stained.*

CAMEL. Scribbled fast, sloping. *Sand becomes waves. Kneels to whisper. Desert bows in prayer.*

The page is crowding, arrows criss-crossing, words colliding.

FACES. *Pressed again, again. Grin rubbed out. Ash blur.*

CANVAS. *Rot under rain-soaked leaves. Pigment leaches. Worms crawl beauty into silence.*

Tin crushed empty. Ink blot spreading.

RUNWAY. Capital letters. *Fire. Applause breaking. Heel splinters. Step after step. No return.*

CROW. Circled, starred, circled again. *One wing torn. One eye gone. Gaze sharp as knife at throat. Knife* scratched out, replaced with *blade.*

PIANO. *Salt-stained keys. Notes drip. Tuned to drowning.*

A pause. Pen hovers. He writes ***CHOCOLATE?*** with a question mark. *Lovers consuming, not kissing.* Scratched through, left to bleed on the page.

Branch taps again. Louder. The pond outside darker, no ripple this time.

TUNNEL. Underlined hard. *Yawns wide. Song at its mouth. No echo. Not train. Only calling.*

TREE. Ink gouged so deep the paper nearly tears. *Bark split. Sap black. Words carved deeper than prayer. Flesh leaning close. Too close.*

Hand cramps. Thumb smudged blue.

Back to the top. He writes it again—***NINETEENTH***. Circle. Star. Underline.

He tries to drag it into being. The pen scratches, stalls, bleeds.

I try to write the nineteenth, but it refuses to form. All I see are headlights in fog, red paint rising through the mist. Not a train. A bus. A double-decker, looming closer, closer.

This could be the one. The nineteenth. The story that—

www.ingramcontent.com/pod-product-compliance
Ingram Content Group UK Ltd.
Pitfield, Milton Keynes, MK11 3LW, UK
UKHW021319061225
465807UK00007B/183